BOOKS BY LOUIS SACHAR

The Wayside School series
Sideways Stories from Wayside School
Wayside School Is Falling Down
Wayside School Gets a Little Stranger
Wayside School Beneath the Cloud of Doom

Holes
There's a Boy in the Girls' Bathroom
Fuzzy Mud

The Marvin Redpost series
Marvin Redpost: Kidnapped at Birth?
Marvin Redpost: Why Pick on Me?
Marvin Redpost: Is He a Girl?
Marvin Redpost: Alone in His Teacher's House
Marvin Redpost: Class President
Marvin Redpost: A Flying Birthday Cake?
Marvin Redpost: Super Fast, Out of Control
Marvin Redpost: A Magic Crystal?

WAYSIDE SCHOOL
IS *FALLING DOWN*

LOUIS SACHAR

Illustrated by **Aleksei Bitskoff**

BLOOMSBURY
CHILDREN'S BOOKS
LONDON OXFORD NEW YORK NEW DELHI SYDNEY

BLOOMSBURY CHILDREN'S BOOKS
Bloomsbury Publishing Plc
50 Bedford Square, London WC1B 3DP, UK
29 Earlsfort Terrace, Dublin 2, Ireland

BLOOMSBURY, BLOOMSBURY CHILDREN'S BOOKS and the Diana logo
are trademarks of Bloomsbury Publishing Plc

First published in the USA in 1989 by Lothrop, Lee and Shepard,
an imprint of HarperCollins
First published in Great Britain in 2004 by Bloomsbury Publishing Plc
This edition published in Great Britain in 2021 by Bloomsbury Publishing Plc

A catalogue record for this book is available from the British Library

ISBN: PB: 978-1-5266-2204-4; eBook: 978-1-5266-3655-3

2 4 6 8 10 9 7 5 3 1

Typeset by RefineCatch Limited, Bungay, Suffolk

Printed and bound in Great Britain by CPI Group (UK) Ltd, Croydon CR0 4YY

MIX
Paper from
responsible sources
FSC® C020471

To find out more about our authors and books visit
www.bloomsbury.com and sign up for our newsletters

To Emily, Walker, Annie, Bill, Bobbie and Corky

CONTENTS

MEET SOME OF THE KIDS IN MRS JEWLS'S CLASS

Todd got in trouble every day ... until he got a magic dog.

Paul can't resist Leslie's Pigtails ... especially since they saved his life.

Ron dared to try the cafeteria's mushroom surprise ... and somehow lived to tell about it.

Myron didn't like being cooped up in a classroom ... so he went down to the basement of Wayside School.

Kathy likes to see bad things happen. Her favourite song is 'Wayside School is falling down.'

Jason had his big mouth taped shut. Now he can't talk, or chew-up all the pencils.

Dameon is in love with his teacher ... so he put a dead rat in her desk drawer.

And it gets worse – because everything is weird at Wayside School!

1

A PACKAGE FOR MRS JEWLS

Louis, the yard teacher, frowned.

The schoolyard was a mess. There were pencils and pieces of paper everywhere. How'd all this junk get here? he wondered. Well, I'm not going to pick it up!

It wasn't his job to pick up garbage. He was just supposed to pass out the balls during lunch and recess, and also make sure the kids didn't kill each other.

He sighed, then began cleaning it up. He loved all the children at Wayside School. He didn't want them playing on a dirty playground.

As he was picking up the pencils and pieces of paper, a large truck drove into the car park. It honked its horn twice, then twice more.

Louis ran to the truck. 'Quiet!' he whispered. 'Children are trying to learn in there!' He pointed at the school.

A short man with big, bushy hair stepped out of the truck. 'I have a package for somebody named Mrs Jewls,' he said.

'I'll take it,' said Louis.

'Are you Mrs Jewls?' asked the man.

'No,' said Louis.

'I have to give it to Mrs Jewls,' said the man.

Louis thought a moment. He didn't want the man disturbing the children. He knew how much they hated to be interrupted when they were working.

'I'm Mrs Jewls,' he said.

'But you just said you weren't Mrs Jewls,' said the man.

'I changed my mind,' said Louis.

The man got the package out of the back of the truck and gave it to Louis. 'Here you go, Mrs Jewls,' he said.

'Uhh!' Louis grunted. It was a very heavy package. The word FRAGILE was printed on every side. He had to be careful not to drop it.

The package was so big, Louis couldn't see where he was going. Fortunately, he knew the way to Mrs Jewls's class by heart. It was straight up.

Wayside School was thirty storeys high, with only one room on each storey. Mrs Jewls's class was at the very top. It was Louis's favourite class.

He pushed through the door to the school, then started up the stairs. There was no lift.

There were stairs that led down to the basement too, but nobody ever went down there. There were dead rats living in the basement.

The box was pressed against Louis's face, squashing his nose. Even so, when he reached the fifteenth floor, he could smell Miss Mush cooking in the cafeteria. It smelt like she was making mushrooms. Maybe on my way back I'll stop by Miss Mush's room and get some mushrooms, he thought. He didn't want to miss Miss Mush's mushrooms. They were her speciality.

He huffed and groaned and continued up the stairs. His arms and legs were very sore, but he didn't want to rest. This package might be important, he thought. I have to get it to Mrs Jewls right away.

He stepped easily from the eighteenth storey to the twentieth. There was no nineteenth storey.

Miss Zarves taught the class on the nineteenth storey. There was no Miss Zarves.

At last he struggled up the final step to the thirtieth storey. He knocked on Mrs Jewls's door with his head.

Mrs Jewls was in the middle of teaching her class about gravity when she heard the knock. 'Come in,' she called.

'I can't open the door,' Louis gasped. 'My hands are full. I have a package for you.'

Mrs Jewls faced the class. 'Who wants to open the door for Louis?' she asked.

All the children raised their hands. They loved to be interrupted when they were working.

'Oh dear, how shall I choose?' asked Mrs Jewls. 'I have to be fair about this. I know! We'll have a spelling bee. And the winner will get to open the door.'

Louis knocked his head against the door again. 'It's heavy,' he complained. 'And I'm very tired.'

'Just a second,' Mrs Jewls called back. 'Allison, the first word's for you. Heavy.'

'Heavy,' said Allison. 'H-E-A-V-Y. Heavy.'

'Very good. Jason, you're next. Tired.'

'Tired,' said Jason. 'S-L-E-E-P-Y. Tired.'

Louis felt the package slipping from his sweaty fingers. He shifted his weight to get a better grip. The corners of the box dug into the sides of his arms. He felt his hands go numb.

Actually, he *didn't* feel them go numb.

'Jenny, package.'

'Package,' said Jenny. 'B-O-X. Package.'

'Excellent!' said Mrs Jewls.

Louis felt like he was going to faint.

At last John opened the door. 'I won the spelling bee, Louis!' he said.

'Very good, John,' muttered Louis.

'Aren't you going to shake my hand?' asked John.

Louis shifted the box to one arm, quickly shook John's hand, then grabbed the box again and staggered into the room.

'Where do you want it, Mrs Jewls?' he asked.

'I don't know,' said Mrs Jewls. 'What is it?'

'I don't know,' said Louis. 'I'll have to put it down someplace so you can open it.'

'But how can I tell you where to put it until I know what it is?' asked Mrs Jewls. 'You might put it in the wrong place.'

So Louis held the box as Mrs Jewls stood on a chair next to him and tore open the top. His legs wobbled beneath him.

'It's a computer!' exclaimed Mrs Jewls.

Everybody booed.

'What's the matter?' asked Louis. 'I thought everyone loved computers.'

'We don't want it, Louis,' said Eric Bacon.

'Take it back, Jack,' said Terrence.

'Get that piece of junk out of here,' said Maurecia.

'Now, don't be that way,' said Mrs Jewls. 'The computer will help us learn. It's a lot quicker than a pencil and paper.'

'But the quicker we learn, the more work we have to do,' complained Todd.

'You may set it over there on the counter, Louis,' said Mrs Jewls.

Louis set the computer on the counter next to Sharie's desk. Then he collapsed on the floor.

'Now watch closely,' said Mrs Jewls.

Everyone gathered around the new computer. It had a full-colour monitor and two disk drives.

Mrs Jewls pushed it out the window.

They all watched it fall and smash on to the pavement.

'See?' said Mrs Jewls. 'That's gravity.'

'Oh, now I get it!' said Joe.

'Thank you, Louis,' said Mrs Jewls. 'I've been trying to teach them about gravity all morning. We had been using pencils and pieces of paper, but the computer was a lot quicker.'

2

MARK MILLER

Mrs Jewls rang her cowbell. 'I would like you to meet Mark Miller,' she said. 'He and his family just moved here all the way from Magadonia!'

Everybody stared at the new kid.

He stood at the front of the room. His knees were shaking.

He hated having to stand in front of the class. It was as if Mrs Jewls had brought him in for show-and-tell. He felt like some kind of weirdo. He just wanted to sit at a desk and be like everybody else.

But worst of all, his name wasn't Mark Miller.

He was Benjamin Nushmutt. And he had moved from Hempleton, not Magadonia.

But he was too scared to mention that to Mrs Jewls. He was afraid to correct a teacher.

'Why don't you tell the class a little bit about yourself, Mark?' suggested Mrs Jewls.

Benjamin didn't know what to say. He wished he really was Mark Miller. Mark Miller wouldn't be scared, he thought. He'd probably have lots to say. Everyone would like him. Nobody would think Mark Miller was weird.

'Well, I guess we'd better find you a place to sit,' said Mrs Jewls.

She put him at the empty desk between Todd and Bebe.

'Hi, Mark,' said Todd. 'I'm Todd. You'll like Mrs Jewls. She's the nicest teacher in the school.'

'Todd, no talking,' said Mrs Jewls. 'Go write your name on the blackboard under the word DISCIPLINE.'

'Hi, Mark,' said Bebe. 'I'm Bebe Gunn.'

'Hi,' Benjamin said quietly.

He decided he'd have to tell Mrs Jewls his real name at recess. He cringed. He didn't know why, but for some reason he had trouble saying his own name.

'And what's your name, little boy?' an adult would ask him.

'Benjamin Nushmutt,' he'd answer.

'What?'

'BENjamin NUSHmutt.'

'What?'

'Ben-Ja-Min Nush-Mutt.'

'What?'

'BenjaMIN NushMUTT!'

'What?'

'Benjamin Nushmutt.'

'Oh, nice to meet you, Benjamin.'

He never knew what it was that made the person suddenly understand.

When the bell rang for recess, everyone charged out of the room. Benjamin slowly walked to Mrs Jewls's desk. Somehow, he had to tell her.

Mrs Jewls was sorting papers. 'Oh, hello, Mark,' she said. 'How are you enjoying the class so far?'

'Fine,' said Benjamin.

'Good, I'm glad to hear that,' said Mrs Jewls.

Benjamin shrugged, then walked out of the room. If I had told her my name, she would have thought I was weird for not telling her sooner, he realised.

He stood at the top of the stairs and looked down. Recess was only ten minutes long. It didn't seem worth it to go all the way down and then come all the way back up. He didn't have any friends down there anyway.

He had never been more unhappy in his whole life.

He sat on the top step. 'Mark Miller,' he said out loud. It was an easy name to say. Mark Miller probably would have made lots of friends by now, he thought.

Suddenly he heard a low rumble. Then the stairs began to shake. It felt like an earthquake! This whole stupid school is going to fall over, he thought. He put his head between his knees.

The rumbling got worse. I'm going to die and nobody will even know who I am, he worried. The new kid. Mark Miller. The weirdo!

But it wasn't an earthquake. It was just all the kids running back up the stairs.

'Hey, Mark, why are you sitting that way?' asked Deedee.

'You look funny,' said Ron.

Benjamin looked up.

'How come you weren't at recess?' asked Jason. 'We looked everywhere for you.'

'Couldn't you find the playground?' asked Calvin.

'It's just straight down,' said Bebe. 'You can't miss it.'

'But don't go in the basement,' warned Sharie. 'Whatever you do, don't go in the basement.'

'We'll go down together at lunch,' said Todd. 'That way you won't get lost.'

Benjamin smiled. He was glad everyone seemed to like him. Or at least they liked Mark Miller. He wondered if they'd like Benjamin Nushmutt too.

'The bell has rung!' said Mrs Jewls, standing in the doorway. 'Now, everyone get inside.' She made Todd put a tick next to his name on the board for being late.

Mrs Jewls handed a stack of work sheets to Dameon and asked him to pass them out to the rest of the class.

Benjamin looked at his work sheet. At the top right corner there was a place to put his name. He didn't know which name to put there, Mark Miller or Benjamin Nushmutt.

He left it blank and started working on the first problem.

Louis, the yard teacher, entered the room carrying a white paper bag. 'Benjamin forgot his lunch,' he said. 'His mother just brought it.'

'Who?' asked Mrs Jewls.

'Benjamin,' said Louis.

'There's no Benjamin in my class,' said Mrs Jewls.

'Are you sure?' asked Louis. 'It looks like a good lunch.'

'I know the names of the children in my class!' Mrs Jewls said indignantly.

'Well, I'll just leave it here until I figure this out,' said Louis. He left the lunch on Mrs Jewls's desk and walked out of the room.

Benjamin frowned. He looked at the white paper bag on Mrs Jewls's desk. He couldn't tell Mrs Jewls his real name now. She'd think he was making it up just to get a free lunch.

He wrote *Mark Miller* at the top of his work sheet.

But one of these days, he knew, he'd have to tell her his real name.

3

BEBE'S BABY BROTHER

Mrs Jewls asked Dameon to pass back the homework.

Bebe Gunn waited nervously. Except for art, her grades had not been very good lately. If she didn't start bringing home better grades, her parents said they wouldn't let her stay up past midnight. She did her best artwork after midnight.

Dameon handed Calvin his homework, then Todd, then Joy.

'Where's yours?' asked Calvin.

'I don't know,' said Bebe.

'Did you do it?' asked Calvin.

'Yes, I did it,' said Bebe. 'I worked extra hard on it! I hope Mrs Jewls didn't lose it.'

Dameon finished passing out the homework. Bebe never got hers.

'Bebe, will you come here, please,' said Mrs Jewls.

She pushed out of her seat, stood up, and nervously walked to Mrs Jewls's desk. 'I did my homework, Mrs Jewls,' she said. 'Really!'

'Yes, I know,' said Mrs Jewls. She held Bebe's homework in her hand.

'Whew!' Bebe sighed with relief. 'I was afraid you lost it!'

'No, I didn't lose it,' Mrs Jewls said sternly. She showed the back of the paper to Bebe. Someone had written:

MRS JEWLS IS AS FAT
AS A HIPPOPOTAMUS!
(AND SHE SMELLS LIKE ONE, TOO.)

'I didn't write that!' exclaimed Bebe. 'I love the way you smell.'

Mrs Jewls smiled. 'But if you didn't write it, who did?'

'Ray!' Bebe instantly replied.

'Who's Ray?'

'He's my little brother. Ray Gunn. He must have snuck into my room after I was asleep. He's always playing mean tricks on me. He knew how hard I worked on my homework.'

'Well, we'll show Ray,' said Mrs Jewls. She gave Bebe an A+. 'There. I don't think he'll try that again.'

'Thanks!' said Bebe.

'You may have a Tootsie Roll Pop, too,' said Mrs Jewls.

Bebe took a Tootsie Roll Pop out of the coffee can on Mrs Jewls's desk, then returned to her seat. She proudly showed Calvin her A+.

The next day Mrs Jewls asked Dameon to hand back another batch of homework.

'How come Dameon always gets to do everything?' griped Kathy.

'I'm sorry, Kathy,' said Mrs Jewls. 'Would you like to pass back the homework?'

'No!' grumped Kathy. 'I'm not your slave.'

Dameon passed out the homework. Again Bebe didn't get hers.

Mrs Jewls called her to her desk. On the back of her homework someone had written:

MRS JEWLS HAS A HEAD FULL OF OATMEAL!
(AND IT LEAKS OUT HER EARS.)

'I didn't write it,' said Bebe.

'Ray?' asked Mrs Jewls.

Bebe nodded.

'Why don't you start checking the back of your homework?' suggested Mrs Jewls.

'I did when I woke up!' said Bebe. 'He must have done it after breakfast, while I was brushing my teeth. We had oatmeal for breakfast.' She shook her head. 'I won't brush my teeth any more!'

'You have to brush your teeth,' said Mrs Jewls.

'My parents think he's such a little angel!' Bebe complained. 'He's always wrecking things, and then I'm always the one who gets in trouble. "Why can't you be more like Ray?" they say. Yesterday he threw all my underwear out the window. Then my mother yelled at me for it. She wouldn't believe that her little darling son would do something like that!'

Mrs Jewls gave Bebe another A+ and another Tootsie Roll Pop.

For Friday everyone had to write a report and read it to the class. Bebe wrote her report about George Washington. She stood at the front of the room and read it out loud.

'... George Washington never told a lie. Not like Mrs Jewls. She lies all the time. That's why her nose is so big. And she snores when she sleeps, so Mister Jewls has to wear ear plugs.'

Everyone was laughing.

Bebe stopped reading. 'What's so funny?' she asked.

'Come here,' said Mrs Jewls.

Bebe shrugged, then walked to Mrs Jewls's desk.

Mrs Jewls showed her what she had just read.

'Did I just read that out loud?' Bebe asked.

Mrs Jewls nodded.

'I was just reading it,' Bebe explained. 'I wasn't listening.'

'It was Ray again, wasn't it?' asked Mrs Jewls.

'Had to be,' said Bebe. 'Yesterday he put toothpaste in my socks. Then my mother got mad at me for making a mess and wasting toothpaste.'

Bebe got an A+ on her report and another Tootsie Roll Pop.

After school Mrs Jewls called Bebe's mother on the phone. 'Hello, Mrs Gunn. This is Mrs Jewls from Wayside School.'

'What's Bebe done now?' asked Mrs Gunn.

'Bebe hasn't done anything wrong,' said Mrs Jewls. 'She's a wonderful girl.'

'Well, that's a surprise!' said Mrs Gunn. 'She's always causing trouble at home.'

'I wanted to talk to you about that,' said Mrs Jewls. 'I think you're being unfair to Bebe. I think she often gets into trouble when really Ray is to blame.'

'Ray?' asked Mrs Gunn.

'Yes. I know you think he's a perfect angel,' said Mrs Jewls, 'but some children can be angels on the outside and devils underneath.'

'Yes, that sounds like Bebe,' said Mrs Gunn.

'I'm not talking about Bebe. I'm talking about Ray.'
'Ray?' asked Bebe's mother. 'Who's Ray?'

4

HOMEWORK

Mrs Jewls was teaching the class about fractions and decimals. She explained that .5 was the same as ½.

Mac raised his hand.

Mrs Jewls pretended not to see him.

'Oooh! Oooh!' Mac groaned as he stretched his hand so high that it hurt.

Mrs Jewls pretended not to hear him.

Jenny raised her hand.

'Yes, Jenny?' said Mrs Jewls, glad to call on anyone besides Mac.

'Mac has his hand raised,' said Jenny.

'Um, thank you, Jenny,' muttered Mrs Jewls. 'Yes, Mac, what is it?'

'I couldn't find one of my socks this morning,' said Mac. 'Man, I looked everywhere! In my closet, in the bathroom, in the kitchen, but I just couldn't find it! I asked my mother, but she hadn't seen it either.'

'That's very interesting, Mac,' Mrs Jewls said patiently, 'but what does that have to do with decimals?'

'Because,' said Mac, 'I only could find *half* of my socks!'

'Oh. Right,' said Mrs Jewls. 'Does anybody else have any questions about decimals? Yes, John?'

'Did you look under the bed?' asked John.

'That was one of the first places I looked,' said Mac, 'but it wasn't there.'

'Did you check the dirty clothes?' asked Ron. 'Maybe it was never washed.'

'I checked,' said Mac.

'Do you have a dog?' asked Bebe. 'Maybe your dog took it.'

'No, my dog doesn't wear socks,' said Mac.

'Why didn't you just put on a different sock?' asked Allison. 'Even if it didn't match?'

'I thought of that,' said Mac. 'See, but then if I wore a sock that didn't match, I'd be left with only one sock of that colour for tomorrow. And then if I wore that sock, I'd have to wear a sock that didn't match with it. And so on for the rest of my life! I would never wear matching socks again.'

'Well, be that as it may,' said Mrs Jewls, 'we really need to get back to decimals. Yes, Stephen?'

'Once I had both my socks on,' said Stephen, 'but I wasn't wearing my shoes. My mom had just waxed the floor, too. I slid all around on it like I was skating. It was a lot of fun until I fell against the kitchen table and broke two dishes. Then I got in trouble.'

'What's *that* got to do with *my* socks?' Mac asked impatiently.

Stephen shrugged.

'Did you ever find your other sock?' asked Leslie.

'Yep,' said Mac, 'but you'll never guess where. In the refrigerator!' He held out his arms in bewilderment. 'How did it get there?'

No one knew.

'See, here it is,' said Mac. He climbed on top of his desk so everyone could see his feet. He pointed to his left foot and said, 'This is the sock I had from the beginning.' He pointed to his right foot and said, 'And this is the sock I couldn't find.'

His socks were red with gold lightning bolts down the side.

'Ooh, hot socks!' said Maurecia.

'No, it was cold after being in the refrigerator,' said Mac, still standing on top of his desk. 'I made it up a song, too, while I was looking for it. You want to hear it?'

He sang:

'I got one sock!
    Lookin' for the other
One sock!
    Lookin' for its brother.
When I find that sock!
    I'll tell you what I'll do.
I'll put it on my foot,
    and I'll stick it in my shoe!'

The bell rang for recess.

'Since we didn't finish the arithmetic lesson,' said Mrs Jewls, 'you'll have to do the rest of it for homework.'

All the kids groaned as they headed outside.

After recess was science. Mrs Jewls was teaching the class about dinosaurs. She told the class that there were two types of dinosaurs: those that ate meat, and those that ate only vegetables.

'You mean like broccoli?' asked Rondi.

'I don't think they had broccoli back then,' said Mrs Jewls. 'Just as there were different kinds of animals back then, there were also different kinds of vegetables.'

Mac raised his hand.

Mrs Jewls pretended not to see him.

'Ooh! Ooh!' Mac groaned. He looked like he was going to explode.

Mrs Jewls pretended not to hear him. She called on Myron.

'Mac has his hand raised,' said Myron.

'Um, thank you, Myron,' muttered Mrs Jewls. 'Yes, Mac?'

'My uncle grew the biggest watermelon you ever saw in your whole life. Man, it was huge! It was so heavy I couldn't even lift it.'

'Mac, what does this have to do with dinosaurs?' asked Mrs Jewls.

'Because that must have been the kind of watermelon that dinosaurs ate,' said Mac.

'Did you eat it?' asked D.J.

'Not all of it,' said Mac, shaking his head. 'Whew, it was too big for me, and I love watermelon!'

'What did it taste like?' asked Maurecia.

'Delicious!' said Mac. 'But lots of seeds. You shouldn't eat the seeds. Otherwise a watermelon might grow inside your stomach. I once heard about a lady who was so fat that everyone thought she was going to have a baby. But she didn't have a baby. She had a watermelon!'

'Was it a boy or a girl?' asked Joy.

Everyone laughed.

Mrs Jewls never finished her lesson about dinosaurs, so she had to assign it for homework.

After school Mac walked home with his girlfriend, Nancy. Nancy's class was on the twenty-third floor of Wayside.

Mac carried his arithmetic book, his science book, his reading book, his language book, and his spelling book.

Nancy didn't have any books. 'I'll carry your books for you, Mac,' she offered.

Mac gave Nancy his books. 'Don't you have any homework?' he asked.

She shook her head.

'Man, it's unfair,' said Mac. 'Mrs Jewls assigns more homework than any other teacher in Wayside School.'

5

ANOTHER STORY ABOUT SOCKS

Sharie brought a hobo to school for show-and-tell.

They stood side by side at the front of the room.

'This is a hobo,' said Sharie. 'I found him on the way to school.'

'Ooh, how neat!' said Maurecia.

The hobo had long dirty hair and a scraggly beard. His shirt was covered with stains. His trousers had lots of colourful patches. His coat was too big for him, but it wasn't as big as Sharie's coat.

Sharie was a little girl, but she wore the biggest coat in all of Wayside School.

The hobo wore old black shoes that also looked like

they were too big for him, but that might have been because he wasn't wearing any socks.

'Tell the class something about your hobo,' said Mrs Jewls.

'His name is Bob,' said Sharie. 'I heard him ask a lady for spare change. The lady told him to take a bath. I tried to give him a quarter, but he said he never took money from kids. He said he likes kids a lot. He said he was once a kid himself.'

'Does anybody have any questions they'd like to ask Hobo Bob?' asked Mrs Jewls.

All the children raised their hands.

The hobo looked around the room. 'Yes, you,' he said, pointing at Jason.

'When's the last time you took a bath?' asked Jason.

'I never take baths,' said the hobo.

'Oh, wow,' said Jason. 'You're lucky!'

'What about a shower?' asked Myron.

'I just walk outside in the rain,' said the hobo.

'When it rains, I have to go inside!' complained Myron.

'Where do you live?' asked Joe.

'All over,' said Bob. 'In the winter I jump on a south-bound train and ride until it's warm enough to jump off. In the summer I go north, where it's not too hot.'

'How come you're not wearing any socks?' asked Leslie.

'I don't believe in socks,' said Bob. 'Yes, the boy in the green shirt.'

'Were you really a kid once?' asked Todd.

'Yep,' said Bob.

'Did you get in trouble a lot?' asked Todd.

'No, I never got in trouble,' said Bob.

Todd smiled and nodded his head.

'Did you like to pull girls' pigtails?' asked Paul.

'Of course,' said Bob. 'Who doesn't?'

'Did you like ice cream?' asked Maurecia.

'I loved it,' said Bob.

'What was your favourite subject?' asked Jenny.

'Spelling,' said the hobo.

'Spelling!' exclaimed Jenny. 'I hate spelling!'

'I once came in first place in a spelling bee, out of all the kids in my school,' Bob said proudly.

'Well, how come you became a hobo?' asked Dameon. 'I mean, if you're such a good speller?'

'I'm not sure,' said Bob. 'When you grow up, you're supposed to turn into something. Some kids turn into dentists. Others turn into bank presidents. I didn't turn into anything. So I became a hobo.'

'Did you ever try to get a job?' asked Calvin.

'I tried,' said Bob. 'But nobody would hire me because I didn't wear socks.'

'So why didn't you just wear socks?' asked Eric Fry.

'I told you. I don't believe in socks. Yes, the girl with the cute front teeth.'

Rondi lowered her hand. She was missing her two front teeth. 'What do you eat?' she asked.

'Mulligan stew,' said Bob. 'My friends and I collect scraps of food all day, and then we cook it up in a big pot and share it. It's always different, but very tasty.'

'Why is it called mulligan stew?' asked Stephen.

'There was once a hobo named Mulligan,' said Bob. 'He made the first mulligan stew.'

'Was he a good cook?' asked Todd.

'No, he was eaten by cannibals.'

'Yuck!' everyone said together, except for Dana, who was very confused. She thought Bob had said he was eaten by cannonballs.

Allison raised her hand. 'Can't you just wear socks, even if you don't believe in them?' she asked.

'Socks!' Bob shouted so loud it scared everybody. 'Is that all you kids ever talk about? Socks! Socks! Socks! Albert Einstein didn't wear any socks! Why should I?'

'Who's Albert Einstein?' asked Eric Ovens.

Mrs Jewls answered that question. She said, 'Albert Einstein was the smartest man who ever lived.'

'Was he also a hobo?' asked D.J.

'No, he was a great scientist,' said Mrs Jewls.

'Why didn't Albert Einstein wear socks?' asked Joy.

'Because socks make you stupid,' said Bob.

'That's not true,' said Mrs Jewls. 'Albert Einstein was just too busy thinking about big important things to remember to put on his socks.'

'Maybe,' said Bob. 'But remember I told you I won the school spelling bee? Well, the day I won it, I forgot to wear socks. Think about it.'

Everyone thought about it.

'So after that I never wore socks again,' said Bob.

 Mac raised his hand. 'Once I could only find one of my socks,' he said. 'Man, I looked everywhere for it! Under the bed, in the bathroom. You'll never guess where I finally found it.'

'In the refrigerator,' said Bob.

Mac's mouth dropped open. 'How'd you know?'

Bob shrugged. 'Where else?'

Everybody had lots more questions for Hobo Bob, but Mrs Jewls rang her cowbell. 'Show-and-tell is over,' she announced. 'Let's all thank Bob.'

'Thank you, Bob,' everyone said together.

'You're welcome,' he replied.

'Do you know the way out of the school?' asked Sharie.

'I'm not sure,' said Bob.

'Just go straight down the stairs,' said Sharie.

'Thank you,' said Bob.

'But don't go in the basement,' warned Sharie.

'I won't,' said Bob. He shook Sharie's hand, then waved goodbye to the rest of the class and headed out the door.

Everybody waved back. Sharie returned to her seat.

It was time for their weekly spelling test. 'Everyone take out a piece of paper and a pencil,' said Mrs Jewls. 'The first word is –'

'Wait a second!' called Calvin. 'I'm not ready yet.'

Mrs Jewls waited while all the children took off their socks.

6
PIGTAILS

'Hi, Leslie,' said Paul.

'Hi, Paul,' said Leslie.

They were friends now. Paul hadn't pulled either of her pigtails for a long time.

Paul sat in the desk behind Leslie. Once, a long time ago, he had pulled Leslie's pigtails. It felt *great*!

That is – Paul thought it felt great. Leslie didn't think it felt too good.

But that was earlier in the year, when Paul was younger and immature. Now he knew better.

Still, her two long brown pigtails hung in front of his face, all day, every day.

The bell rang for recess.

'Leslie,' said Paul. 'Can I talk to you a second?'

'Sure, Paul,' said Leslie.

They were alone in the room. All the other kids had rushed down the stairs. Mrs Jewls had run to the teachers' lounge.

'I've been good, right?' asked Paul. 'I haven't pulled one of your pigtails in a long time, have I?'

'So what do you want, a medal?' asked Leslie.

Paul chuckled. 'No, well, can I ask you something?'

'Sure,' said Leslie.

Paul took a breath. 'May I pull just one of your pigtails?' he asked. 'Please?'

'No!' said Leslie.

'Please?' Paul begged. 'I won't pull it hard. No one will have to know. Please? Please? I wouldn't ask if it wasn't important! Please?'

'You're sick!' exclaimed Leslie.

Paul lowered his head. 'I'm sorry,' he said. 'You're right. I don't know what came over me. I won't ask again.'

'Good,' said Leslie. She shook her head in disgust.

Paul watched her pigtails waggle. 'Can I just touch one?' he asked. 'I won't even pull it. I promise.'

'No!'

'What's wrong with just touching one?' Paul asked.

'Yuck, you're gross!' said Leslie as she turned and marched out of the room.

As Paul watched her go, her pigtails seemed to wave goodbye to him.

He slapped himself in the face with both hands. What's wrong with me? he wondered.

He walked to the side of the room and leaned over the counter. He stuck his head out the window to get some fresh air. Down below, he could see the kids playing on the playground. They looked like tiny toys.

Leslie stepped back into the classroom. 'I'm getting my hair trimmed tomorrow,' she announced. 'If you want, I'll save the pieces for you. It'll just be some split ends.'

Paul was so excited he forgot where he was. He quickly raised his head. It bashed against the window frame, then he bounced forward and toppled out the window.

Leslie stared in horror at the open window, then rushed towards it. She leaned over the counter and looked down.

'Help!' gasped Paul.

There was one brick on the side of the building that stuck out a little further than the others. Paul desperately held on to it with both hands.

'I'll go get Louis,' said Leslie. 'He'll save you.'

'No, don't go!' cried Paul. 'I can't hold on. My fingers are slipping!'

Leslie reached down for him. 'Try to grab my hand,' she said.

Paul made a grab for it, but missed, then quickly clutched the brick. 'I can't! Help, I'm scared.'

'Just don't look down,' said Leslie as she tried to stay calm. She pulled her head back in through the window.

'Where are you going!' cried Paul. 'Help! Don't leave me.'

Leslie looked around Mrs Jewls's room for a rope or an extension cord or something for Paul to grab, but she couldn't find anything.

She returned to the window, sighed, then leaned out backwards. Her hands tightly held the edge of the counter as she looked up at the sky. 'Grab my pigtails,' she said, then winced.

A big smile came across Paul's face. 'Really?' he asked.

'Just do it!' said Leslie.

The pigtails hung about a foot above Paul's head. He let go of the brick with his right hand and grabbed her right pigtail.

'Yaaaaaaaaahhhhhhhhh!' Leslie yelped.

He grabbed her left pigtail with his left hand.

'Yaaaaaaaaaaaaaaahhhhhhhhh!' she screamed.

'OK, pull me in,' said Paul. His legs dangled beneath him.

Leslie's eyes watered in pain as she tried to step away from the window. 'I can't!' she groaned. 'You're too heavy.'

Paul swung his legs up against the side of the building. 'Try now.'

Leslie groaned, then took a small step away from the window as Paul took a small step up the wall. Then they each took another small step. At last Paul managed to get one foot on top of the brick that jutted out.

Leslie pulled her head inside the window. As she took another step, Paul let go of one pigtail and grabbed the windowsill. Leslie took another step, pulling Paul the rest of the way through.

They both collapsed on the floor, tired and sore.

'Ooh, my head hurts,' said Leslie.

'Wow, you saved my life,' said Paul. 'Well, don't worry, some day I'll save yours.'

'You don't have to,' said Leslie. 'Just don't pull my pigtails any more.'

'I won't,' said Paul. Suddenly he laughed.

'What's so funny?' asked Leslie.

'This time your pigtails pulled me.'

7

FREEDOM

Myron crumbled a cracker on the windowsill next to his desk, then looked away. He knew Oddly came only when nobody was looking.

A little while later a bird landed on the windowsill and ate the crumbs. Myron watched him out of the corner of his eye.

He was a black bird with a pink breast. Myron had named him 'Oddly.' Myron had named him oddly.

'Is that your dumb bird again?' asked Kathy.

'No,' said Myron. 'Oddly is not my bird. I don't own him. He doesn't live in a cage. Oddly is free!'

'You're a birdbrain,' said Kathy.

Myron watched Oddly fly away. It made him sad and

glad at the same time. He wished he could fly away across the sky with Oddly.

Oddly probably thinks I live in a cage, he realised. Whenever he sees me, I'm sitting in this same desk. He probably thinks this desk is my cage!

So Myron got out of his chair and sat on the floor.

'Myron, what are you doing out of your seat?' asked Mrs Jewls.

'I want to sit on the floor,' said Myron.

Several kids laughed.

'Get back in your seat,' ordered Mrs Jewls.

Myron reluctantly returned to his desk.

I *do* live in a cage, he thought. I'm not allowed out. I have to stay in my cage until the bell rings. Then I have to go down the stairs. Then when it rings again, I have to go up the stairs. Then when it rings again, I have to go down the stairs. Then when it rings again, I have to go up the stairs. I'm never free.

The bell rang.

Myron went down the stairs.

It was so crowded with kids rushing to recess that he couldn't stop if he wanted. It was as if someone had lifted his cage and was carrying him down the stairs.

The bell rang again.

Myron went up the stairs.

At lunch the bell rang again.

Myron went down the stairs.

After lunch the bell rang again.

Myron stood at the bottom of the staircase and looked up. 'No!' he declared. 'I won't go. I have to be free!'

As all the other kids rushed past him, he eased his way around to the back of the stairs. As everybody else went up, Myron went down …

to

the

basement.

He nervously walked down the old creaky staircase. He didn't know what he'd find, or what would find him. He had heard that dead rats were living down there, or worse, maybe even Mrs Gorf!

Mrs Gorf was the meanest teacher Myron had ever had. She used to be the teacher on the thirtieth storey, before Mrs Jewls took over. But nobody believed that Mrs Gorf was really gone. Everyone said she was still lurking somewhere inside Wayside School.

He stepped off the last step, at the very bottom of Wayside School. It was too dark to see. Somewhere he heard a drip that echoed all around the cold and damp room.

With his arms outstretched, he stepped across the

gritty floor. His hand struck against a large, fat pipe above his head. The pipe felt like it was covered with a thousand spiderwebs. Still, Myron kept his finger on the pipe as he walked, so he wouldn't get lost. As long as he stayed with the pipe, he knew he'd be able to find his way back to the stairs.

Something crawled across his hand. He shook it off, then continued walking.

He thought he heard footsteps behind him. He stopped walking. The sound of the footsteps continued for a second, then stopped.

He started again, then stopped. The footsteps stopped a few seconds later.

He wasn't alone.

It was too dark for Myron to see who was following him, but he realised that meant that the person couldn't see him either. Whoever was coming after him had to have been following along the pipe, too.

So Myron left the safety of the pipe and headed blindly across the basement.

The footsteps continued behind him.

He stopped.

The footsteps stopped, too.

He bent down, then untied and took off his right sneaker. He threw it towards the other side of the basement. He heard it hit on the floor, then the footsteps started after it.

Very quietly, he took off his other sneaker and threw it in the same direction.

He never heard his shoe hit the ground.

The footsteps started after him again.

He started to run, but slipped in his socked feet on a spot of slime. His hands hit loud and hard as he fell on the cold floor.

The footsteps came hurriedly towards him.

He held his breath and tried to be as quiet as possible.

A light turned on above his head.

He screamed.

'I believe this is yours,' said a bald man. He was holding Myron's left sneaker.

Next to him were two men with black moustaches. One of the men held a black briefcase.

Myron shook his head. 'That's not my shoe,' he said. 'I never saw it before.'

The bald man glanced at Myron's shoeless feet.

'What's your name?' asked the man with the briefcase.

'Myron,' said Myron. He regretted it as soon as he had said it. He wished he had made up a fake name.

The man opened his briefcase and took out a note-book. 'Myron,' he repeated, as he thumbed through the notebook. 'You're supposed to be in Mrs Jewls's class, at the desk next to the window, in front of Sharie.'

'What are you doing out of your cage – I mean, seat?' asked the other man with a moustache.

'I just wanted to be free,' chirped Myron. 'Please don't hurt me. If you let me go back to Mrs Jewls's room, I'll never come down here again.'

'Well, do you want to be free, or do you want to be safe?' asked the bald man.

'Huh?' asked Myron.

'You can't have it both ways,' said the bald man.

'Do you want to be safe?' asked one of the men with a moustache. 'Do you want to sit in the same chair every day, and go up and down the stairs every time the bell rings?'

'You'll have go to school five days a week,' said the other man with a moustache. 'And you'll have to go to bed at the same time every day.'

'But first you'll have to brush your teeth,' said the other man with a moustache.

'And you won't be allowed to watch TV until you finish your homework,' said the other man with a moustache.

'You'll have to go inside when it rains,' said the other man with a moustache.

'But first you'll have to wipe your feet,' said the other man with a moustache.

'Or you can be free,' said the bald man.

The man took a pencil and a piece of paper out of his

briefcase. 'So do you want to be safe, or do you want to be free?'

Myron looked at the three men. 'I want to be free,' he said bravely.

The man with the briefcase wrote something on the piece of paper and gave it to Myron. 'Sign here,' he said.

Myron couldn't read the piece of paper. It was written in some kind of foreign language. He signed his name.

The man took the paper and pencil from Myron and put them back into his briefcase. 'OK, you're free,' he said.

'Good luck, Myron,' said the bald man. 'Here, I think you'll need this.' He gave Myron his left sneaker, then reached up and pulled the chain. The light turned off.

Myron found himself alone in the darkness. He put his shoe back on, then hopped across the basement floor. He had no idea how to get back.

At last his hand hit against a pipe. But he still didn't know which way to follow it, left or right. He didn't even know if it was the right pipe. He turned left and continued hopping, keeping his finger on the pipe.

He was just about ready to turn around and try the other way when he nearly fell over the bottom stair.

He hopped up the stairs, and continued hopping all the way up to Mrs Jewls's room.

He was tired, sore, and dirty.

'You're late, Myron,' said Mrs Jewls. 'Go write your name under DISCIPLINE, then return to your seat for the arithmetic test.'

But Myron didn't feel like taking an arithmetic test. And he definitely didn't want to write his name on the board.

So he sat on the floor.

And there was nothing Mrs Jewls could do about it.

He was free.

After school Mrs Jewls found Myron's other sneaker in the teachers' lounge, in the refrigerator.

8

THE BEST PART

Todd brought a toy to school. It was a cute, adorable puppy dog. Everyone who saw it said, 'Aw.'

'Aw,' said Jenny. 'He has such a sweet face.'

'Aw,' said Stephen. 'Look at her darling eyes.'

'Aw,' said Deedee. 'Isn't he the cutest puppy you've ever seen?'

'Aw,' said Calvin. 'Isn't she adorable?'

Joy sat at the desk behind Todd. Big deal, she thought. It's just a hunk of plastic that happens to look like a dog.

But even though Joy didn't like Todd's toy, she decided to steal it.

'Wait,' said Todd. 'Let me show you the best part.'

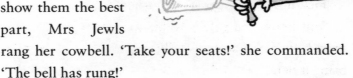

Before he could show them the best part, Mrs Jewls rang her cowbell. 'Take your seats!' she commanded. 'The bell has rung!'

All the children returned to their desks.

'Todd, go write your name on the blackboard.'

Todd was the only one who had been in his seat, yet he was the one who got in trouble. That was typical.

Mrs Jewls had a system. The first time someone got in trouble, he had to write his name on the blackboard under the word DISCIPLINE. The second time he got in trouble, he had to put a tick next to his name. And if he got in trouble a third time, he had to circle his name and then go home early, at twelve o'clock, on the kindergarten bus.

Todd went home on the kindergarten bus every day. Some of the other kids thought he was lucky, but he wished just once he could make it to twelve o'clock without getting into trouble three times.

He walked to the front of the room and wrote his name on the blackboard under the word DISCIPLINE.

While Todd was at the board, Joy reached over her desk and into Todd's. She felt around for the toy. But as she tried to lift it out, it caught on something and dropped to the floor.

Todd returned to his seat.

'Todd, is that your toy on the floor?' asked Mrs Jewels.

'Hey, how'd that get there?' asked Todd.

'You know the rules, Todd,' said Mrs Jewls. 'Toys must be kept inside your desk, or else I take them. Now bring it here.'

Todd gave his toy to Mrs Jewls.

'Awwww, how precious,' cooed Mrs Jewls. 'He's the most lovable puppy I've ever seen.' She kissed Todd's plastic puppy on its plastic nose. 'I guess I can let you off this time,' she said. 'But try to keep him in your desk.' She kissed Todd's toy again, then handed it back to him. 'You can erase your name from the board, too.'

Todd could hardly believe it. For the first time ever, he erased his name from the board.

As he headed back to his seat, Mrs Jewls said, 'Here, take a Tootsie Roll Pop too, for the sweeeeeet puppy.'

Todd was amazed.

So was Joy. Now, more than ever, she wanted that toy!

Out at recess everyone wanted to see Todd's toy.

'It's magic,' said Bebe. 'It kept you from getting into trouble.'

'No, Mrs Jewls is just a nice teacher,' said

47

Todd. 'Here, let me show you the best part.'

He grabbed hold of the dog's tail and turned it like a crank. Suddenly the cute floppy ears stood straight up. The mouth opened wide, and the teeth grew into sharp fangs.

'Wow,' breathed Deedee.

Todd wasn't finished. He pulled the dog's nose and stretched out its face. The cheeks became thin and bony. The eyes were no longer sweet, but grim and frightening.

'What a great toy!' said Calvin.

The cute little puppy had turned into a mean, hungry, man-eating wolf.

'I still haven't shown you the best part,' said Todd. But before he could show them the best part, the bell rang, and everyone ran up the stairs to class.

I've got to get that puppy dog, thought Joy as she stared at the back of Todd's neck. Then I'll never get in trouble again! She didn't know Todd's toy had changed into a man-eating wolf.

Her lunch box was on her lap. She quietly opened it and took out a carton of cranberry juice and a tiny straw.

She stuck the straw into the carton and sucked up some juice into it.

She waited for Mrs Jewls to turn around, then blew the juice out of the straw. It splattered against Todd's neck.

He slapped the back of his neck with his hand.

Joy laughed to herself. She sucked up some more juice, took careful aim, and fired.

Todd turned around, but Joy already had the straw out of her mouth and was looking down at her book.

Todd rubbed his neck and faced front.

Joy sucked up more juice and blew it on to Todd's neck.

'Hey!' he shouted, turning around.

'Leave me alone, Todd – I'm trying to work,' said Joy.

'Todd, what's the matter with you?' asked Mrs Jewls. 'I try to be nice, but you just take advantage. Now go write your name on the blackboard.'

Todd walked to the front of the room. He still thought Mrs Jewls was the nicest teacher in the world. He looked up at the clock. It was almost eleven. I might just make it today, he thought. I just might make it. He started to write his name when he heard a loud scream.

He turned around and saw Joy jumping up and down and waving her hand in the air. His toy was biting her pinky, and she couldn't shake it off.

'Help!' screamed Joy as she hopped around the room. 'Todd, how do I get it off? Todd? Please?'

Todd smiled. 'There,' he said. 'That's the best part.'

9

MUSH

WARNING: Do not read this story right after eating. In fact, don't read it right before eating, either. In fact, just to be safe, don't read this story if you're ever planning to eat again.

Miss Mush wiped her hands on her apron. She smiled at the children who were lined up at the cafeteria. It warmed her heart to see how much they liked her food.

Maurecia was first in line.

'And what would you like today, Maurecia?' Miss Mush asked. She knew the name of every child in Wayside School.

Maurecia looked at the sign.

```
SPECIAL TODAY
Mushroom Surprise
```

'Just milk,' said Maurecia. 'I brought my lunch.' Miss Mush smiled and gave Maurecia a carton of milk.

Joy was next in line.

'And what would you like, Joy?' asked Miss Mush.

'Milk,' said Joy.

Miss Mush smiled and gave Joy a carton of milk. 'And what would you like, Jason?'

'Milk, please,' said Jason.

'Just milk,' said Dameon.

'Milk,' said D.J.

'Milk,' said Leslie.

It was almost Ron's turn. He hadn't brought a lunch. He normally brought a peanut butter and jelly sandwich to school, but there hadn't been a single slice of bread in his house this morning.

'I know!' his mother had said. 'I'll give you some money and you can buy a nice hot lunch from Miss Mush!' She thought it was a brilliant idea.

'Can't I just have a peanut butter and jelly sandwich without the bread?' Ron had asked.

Now he looked up at the sign.

He wished he weren't so hungry.

This was the eighteenth day in a row that the special was Mushroom Surprise. It was called Mushroom Surprise because it would have been a surprise if anybody had ever ordered it. No one ever did – except Louis, of course. That's why they'd had it for eighteen days. There was always plenty left over.

'Milk,' said Terrence.

'Milk,' said Sharie.

'Milk,' said Calvin.

'Milk, please,' said Bebe.

'And what would you like today, Ron?' asked Miss Mush.

Ron took a breath. 'Mushroom Surprise,' he squeaked.

Tears of joy filled Miss Mush's eyes. She blew her nose on her apron, then said, 'One Mushroom Surprise, coming right up!'

Tears came to Ron's eyes too, but for a different reason. He looked at the Mushroom Surprise. It was sort of green.

So was Ron.

Miss Mush proudly dumped a hot lump of Mushroom Surprise on a paper plate and handed it to Ron. He put it on his tray, then pushed it over to the cash register, where he paid for it.

The news quickly spread around the cafeteria, then up and down the stairs and out to the playground.

'Ron ordered the Mushroom Surprise!'

'Ron ordered the Mushroom Surprise!'

Mrs Jewls was sitting in the teachers' lounge on the twelfth floor when Bebe burst into the room.

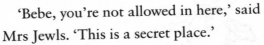

All the teachers were shocked to see her.

'Bebe, you're not allowed in here,' said Mrs Jewls. 'This is a secret place.'

'Ron ordered the Mushroom Surprise!' Bebe shouted; then she ran back up to the cafeteria.

As Ron sat down at a table, eighty-seven kids crowded around him to watch him eat.

'I wonder what the surprise is,' said Deedee. She had the best view. She was pushed right up alongside Ron's chair.

'Maybe it tastes good,' said Leslie.

'Maybe that's the surprise.'

'No, I think it's called Mushroom Surprise because after you eat it, it's a surprise if you don't die,' said Mac.

'Louis eats it. He's not dead,' said Jason.

'Louis has been eating Miss Mush's food for so long, he's immune to it,' said Allison.

Ron dug his plastic fork into the goop. He raised it to his mouth.

Dana covered her eyes. 'I can't watch!' she exclaimed.

Ron opened his mouth wide. The fork entered. He brought the fork out again.

It was empty!

Ron chewed twice, then swallowed.

'He ate it!' Deedee announced for those who couldn't see.

Stephen screamed.

'Hmm,' said Ron. 'Not too bad. It sort of tastes like a mixture of bananas and spinach.'

'What's the surprise?' asked Deedee.

Ron looked at Deedee. His face flushed and his eyes changed colour. His whole body began to shake, like a washing machine on the spin cycle.

Deedee was afraid he was going to throw up. She tried

to get away, but with everyone crowded around, there was no room for her to move.

But Ron didn't throw up. He stood up, put his arms around Deedee's neck, and kissed her smack on the lips.

He sat back down. His eyes returned to their normal colour.

'Ylah!' said Deedee, wiping her mouth on her sleeve.

'What's the matter?' asked Ron.

'Don't you know what you just did?' asked Allison.

He shrugged. 'I ate some Mushroom Surprise. It wasn't bad. Sort of like a mixture of a hot dog and grape jelly. I wonder what the surprise is.'

He dug his plastic fork back into the goop. Everybody ran away.

When Mrs Jewls entered the cafeteria, no one was there except for Ron. He was sitting alone at a table eating Mushroom Surprise.

Mrs Jewls sat down next to him. 'Hi, Ron,' she said. 'So how does it taste? And what's the surprise?'

Ron swallowed another mouthful. He looked at his teacher. His face flushed and his eyes changed colour …

10
MUSIC

Benjamin still hadn't told anybody he wasn't Mark Miller.

His grades had never been better. Mark Miller is a lot smarter than Benjamin Nushmutt, he thought.

When they chose up teams for kickball, he was always the first one picked. Mark Miller is a better kicker than Benjamin Nushmutt, he realised.

The girls in the class liked him too. Mark Miller is better looking than Benjamin Nushmutt, he decided.

But unfortunately, he knew he had to tell Mrs Jewls his real name. He sighed, then slowly raised his hand.

Mrs Jewls gave him a tambourine.

He had been so busy thinking about his problem, he hadn't noticed that Mrs Jewls was passing out musical instruments. She had just asked, 'Who would like the tambourine?' So when he raised his hand, she gave it to him.

'Who would like the triangle?' asked Mrs Jewls. Joe raised his hand, and Mrs Jewls gave it to him.

'Why is it called a triangle?' asked Joe.

'I don't know,' said Mrs Jewls.

'Maybe because it's shaped like a triangle,' suggested John.

'No, that can't be it,' said Mrs Jewls. 'Then the tambourine would have to be called a circle.'

'Maybe it was invented by a person named Joe Triangle,' said Rondi.

'That's probably it,' said Mrs Jewls. She held up the next instrument. It was a glockenspiel. 'Who would like the glockenspiel?' she asked.

Sharie raised her hand.

Nobody asked why it was called a glockenspiel. It was obvious.

Mrs Jewls gave the bells to Stephen.

'Why are they called bells?' he asked. Nobody knew.

Joy got the bongo drums. Todd got the bass drum. Jenny snared the snare drum.

And Leslie got the kettledrum.

When they banged on them, it hurt everybody else's eardrums.

Mrs Jewls gave one cymbal to Calvin and the other cymbal to Bebe.

D.J. got the gong. The three Erics got kazoos.

Mrs Jewls shouted, *'Uno, dos, tres, cuatro!'*

The children all played their instruments. They shook, rattled, rocked, and rolled.

Joy bonged her bongos. D.J. gonged his gong. Sharie glockened her glockenspiel. Stephen jingled his bells. Calvin and Bebe slapped their cymbals together. And Joe's triangle went *ting*.

But something didn't sound right.

'What's wrong, Mark?' Mrs Jewls shouted over the music. 'Why aren't you playing the tambourine?'

'My name's not Mark,' said Benjamin. 'It's Benjamin Nushmutt. I'm sorry for not telling you before.'

'What?' asked Mrs Jewls. 'I can't hear you.'

'My name isn't Mark!' he said. 'It's Benjamin.'

'Louder!' said Mrs Jewls.

So everyone played louder.

Todd bashed his bass drum. Leslie cooked on her kettledrum. Calvin and Bebe crashed their cymbals together. And Joe's triangle went *ting*.

'My name is Benjamin!' shouted Benjamin.

Mrs Jewls put her hand to her ear. 'Louder!' she said.

So everyone played louder.

D.J. kabonged his gong. Joy chongoed her bongos. Paul splacked his castanets. Jenny spaghettied her snare drum. Calvin and Bebe wammered their cymbals. And Joe's triangle went *ting*.

'My name's Benjamin Nushmutt,' hollered Benjamin Nushmutt.

'Louder!' yelled Mrs Jewls.

So everyone played louder.

The three Erics screamed into their kazoos. Calvin and Bebe ran to opposite sides of the room with their cymbals, then charged towards each other.

Suddenly the door flew open, and a man entered. Benjamin had never seen him before.

The whole class became very quiet.

It was Mr Kidswatter, the principal.

Calvin and Bebe screeched to a halt just in time. Their cymbals were less than an inch apart.

'Is something the matter, Mr Kidswatter?' asked Mrs Jewls.

'Several teachers have complained about your music,'

said Mr Kidswatter. 'Their students are having trouble hearing.'

'I understand,' said Mrs Jewls.

'Good,' said Mr Kidswatter. He walked out of the room.

'OK, you heard Mr Kidswatter,' said Mrs Jewls. 'We'll have to play louder so everyone can hear. *Uno, dos, tres, cuatro!*'

They shook, rattled, rocked, and rolled.

Benjamin frampled his tambourine.

'Excellent, Mark!' shouted Mrs Jewls.

He smiled. He had never played so well before. Mark Miller is a better musician than Benjamin Nushmutt, he thought.

11

KATHY AND D.J.

Down on the playground Kathy was singing her favourite song.

'Wayside School is falling down,
  falling down, falling down.
Wayside School is falling down,
  my fair lady.

'Kids go splat as they hit the ground,
  hit the ground, hit the ground.
Kids go splat as they hit the ground,
  my fair lady.'

D.J. was walking across the playground with his head down.

'Hi, Dr Jolly,' said Louis. Louis called D.J. 'Doctor Jolly' because he was always smiling.

But now D.J.'s smile was upside down. He looked up at Louis.

Louis had never seen such a sad face. 'What's wrong?' he asked.

D.J. just shook his head, then looked back down at the ground and sadly walked away.

Louis felt like crying.

'Hey, Louis, what's wrong with D.J.?' asked Ron.

'He's so sad!' said Deedee.

'I don't know,' said Louis, shaking his head. 'Hey, you guys want to play kickball?'

'No thanks,' said Deedee. 'I can't have fun when D.J. is unhappy.'

'Me neither,' said Ron.

Across the playground, all the children quit their games when they saw D.J. Nobody could have fun when D.J. looked so sad.

Except Kathy! She sang:

'Broken bones and blood and gore,
   blood and gore, blood and gore.
Broken bones and blood and gore,
   my fair lady.

'We don't have no school no more,
        school no more, school no more.
    We don't have no school no more,
        my fair lady.'

The bell rang. D.J. sadly looked up at the school and sighed.

'Hey, Deej, snap out of it,' said Myron. D.J. stared through his friend.

'You want to walk up the stairs with us, Dojo?' asked Dameon.

D.J. shook his head. 'I need to be alone,' he mumbled.

Dameon and Myron looked at each other, then started up the stairs, leaving their sad friend behind.

D.J. headed on up, but stopped halfway between the ninth and tenth floors and sat down. He lowered his face into his hands and cried.

A moment later someone burst out laughing.

D.J. opened his eyes and saw Kathy standing over him.

'You shouldn't sit on the stairs, Dumb Jerk!' said Kathy with glee. 'I almost kicked you in the head.' Kathy always called D.J. 'Dumb Jerk.'

She didn't like D.J. because he was always smiling. Now she was glad to see him so sad.

'Hi, Kathy,' said D.J.

She plopped down on the stair next to him. 'What happened?' she asked. 'Did your dog die?' She laughed.

D.J. shook his head.

'Are your parents getting divorced?' she asked hopefully. 'Did your house burn down?'

'No,' said D.J. 'My great-grandfather gave me a gold watch. It was over a hundred years old. I brought it to school today and –'

'You lost it!' Kathy exclaimed with delight.

D.J. sadly nodded.

Kathy laughed. 'Oh boy, are you going to get in trouble!' She rubbed her hands together. 'Your parents will ground you forever!'

'No, my parents never punish me,' said D.J. 'They know I learn from my mistakes.'

'Oh,' said Kathy, a little disappointed. 'But your great-grandfather will *hate* you!' she said. 'And he'll never give you another present for the rest of your life. Not even for your birthday!'

'No, he loves me no matter what I do,' said D.J. 'He likes people, not *things*.'

Again Kathy was disappointed. 'But the watch was wor th a lot of money,' she tried. 'And *you'll* have to pay for it out of *your* allowance.' She laughed triumphantly, sure she had got him this time.

'I don't get an allowance,' said D.J. 'I don't like money.'

Kathy frowned. Still, she knew there had to be some reason why he was sad about losing the watch. 'You'll never know what time it is!' she squawked.

'So?' asked D.J. 'Time isn't real.'

Kathy didn't know what D.J. meant by that, but she didn't care. 'Well, if you don't know what time it is,' she told him, 'you'll miss all your favourite television shows.'

'I don't have a favourite television show,' said D.J. 'I never watch television.' He thought a moment. 'I'm not sure if we have a TV in our house or not. Maybe there's one in a closet somewhere.'

Kathy glared at him. 'Well, then how come you're so sad you lost that dumb watch?' she demanded.

'I'm afraid a bird might think it's food and choke on it,' said D.J.

'Is that all?' shrieked Kathy.

D.J. smiled. 'I guess you're right,' he said. 'A bird probably wouldn't choke. In fact, maybe he could use it to make a nest. I hope so, don't you?' He hopped to his feet. 'Thanks for talking to me, Kathy. I feel a lot better now. You're a good friend.'

He hurried up to Mrs Jewls's room, taking the stairs two and three at a time.

As D.J.'s smile turned up, Kathy's smile turned down. She followed up after him, grumbling to herself. 'He doesn't like money. He doesn't worry about time. He never watches television. Why is he always so happy?'

Everyone in Mrs Jewls's class cheered when they saw D.J. enter the room smiling.

Kathy walked in behind him frowning.

Mrs Jewls was getting ready to show a movie. She gave D.J. a piece of black construction paper.

'Hey, look!' exclaimed Myron. 'Oddly found a watch!'

Oddly, the bird, dropped the watch on the windowsill.

Kathy couldn't believe it! 'It's D.J.'s,' she griped.

Myron gave the watch to D.J.

'Here, you can have it, Kathy,' said D.J. with a big smile. 'It's worth a lot of money, and this way you won't miss any of your favourite television shows.'

Kathy took the watch from him and put it around her wrist. 'It'll probably make my skin turn green,' she groused.

Mrs Jewls started the movie projector. Stephen turned off the lights. Dameon pulled down the blinds. D.J. held the piece of black construction paper under his nose, because his smile was so bright.

12
PENCILS

Jason borrowed a pencil from Allison. When he gave it back to her, it was full of teeth marks.

Allison held the pencil by its point. 'Yuck!' she said. 'You chewed on it.'

Jason felt awful. It is very embarrassing to borrow somebody's pencil and then chew on it. 'Sorry,' he said. 'I didn't do it on purpose.'

'You can keep it,' said Allison. She dropped the pencil on Jason's desk, then raised her hand. 'Mrs Jewls, can I go to the bathroom?

I have to wash my hands. Jason slobbered all over my pencil.'

Everybody laughed.

Jason turned red. 'I'm sorry, Allison,' he said. 'I know it's a disgusting habit. I just can't help it.'

'Don't let Jason touch any of my books,' said Allison as she headed out of the room. 'He might eat them!'

Everybody laughed again.

'Here, you can eat my book, Jason,' said Todd. 'I don't like it anyway.'

Mrs Jewls made Todd write his name on the blackboard under the word DISCIPLINE.

Jason was so mad at himself, he broke the chewed-up pencil to bits.

That wasn't a smart thing to do.

'Everybody take out a pencil and a piece of paper,' said Mrs Jewls. 'It's time for our spelling test.'

Jason slapped himself on the forehead. I'm so stupid! he thought. 'Rondi, may I borrow a pencil, please?' he asked.

Rondi made a face. 'All my pencils are new,' she said. 'How do I know you won't eat it?'

'I won't,' said Jason. 'I promise.'

'You better not,' said Rondi. She gave him one of her pencils.

It was new and freshly sharpened. Jason liked the way it smelt.

'The first word is "orchestra,"' said Mrs Jewls.

Jason tried to remember how to spell *orchestra*. He stuck the back of the pencil in his mouth.

'Second word, "garbanzo."'

Jason chewed on the eraser.

When the spelling test was over, Rondi's pencil was worse than Allison's.

Jason looked at it in horror. He didn't even remember chewing it. Oh, no! he thought. What am I going to do? He stuck it inside his desk.

'Jason, may I have my pencil back, please?' asked Rondi.

'What pencil?' asked Jason.

'The one I lent you,' said Rondi.

Jason opened his desk and pretended to look for it. 'I don't know where it is,' he said.

'Mrs Jewls, Jason stole my pencil!' called Rondi.

'Jason, give Rondi back her pencil,' said Mrs Jewls.

He gave it to her.

'You chewed on it!' exclaimed Rondi.

Everyone laughed.

'No I didn't,' said Jason. 'Those are your teeth marks.'

'How can they be my teeth marks?' asked Rondi. She smiled. She was missing her two front teeth.

'So?' said Jason. 'You don't chew pencils with your front teeth. You chew them with your back teeth.'

'How do you know?' asked Rondi.

'Um, um, uh,' said Jason.

Mrs Jewls made Jason write his name on the board under the word DISCIPLINE because he chewed Rondi's pencil, then lied about it. 'And try not to eat the chalk,' she said.

Everyone laughed.

Rondi threw the chewed-up pencil out the window.

It hit Louis on the head.

Mrs Jewls gave Dameon a stack of work sheets and asked him to pass them out. They contained arithmetic problems.

Jason had to borrow another pencil.

'Allison, may I borrow another pencil, please?' he asked.

'Eat my socks,' said Allison.

That wasn't such a bad idea, Jason realised. If he stuffed a sock in his mouth, he wouldn't be able to chew a pencil.

Myron looked at his work sheet. 'I don't feel like doing this stuff,' he said. 'Here, Jason, you can have my pencil.'

'Thanks, Myron,' said Jason. 'I promise not to chew it.' He hoped he'd be able to keep his promise.

He thought about asking Mrs Jewls for a Tootsie Roll Pop. If I'm sucking on that, I won't chew Myron's pencil. And a Tootsie Roll Pop would probably taste better than

Allison's socks. He didn't know for sure because he had never tasted Allison's socks.

But before he could ask Mrs Jewls, Mrs Jewls called him. 'Jason, will you come here for a moment,' she said. 'I think I know how to keep you from chewing pencils.'

Jason smiled as he walked to her desk. 'I like the purple ones,' he told her.

But Mrs Jewls didn't give him a Tootsie Roll Pop. Instead, she taped his mouth shut with heavy-duty masking tape. She had to use a lot of tape, because Jason had the second biggest mouth in the class. 'There,' she said.

Jason started back to his seat.

'Aren't you even going to say thank you?' asked Mrs Jewls.

'Mhhmm hhm,' said Jason.

'You're welcome,' said Mrs Jewls.

'Hey, Jason,' teased Allison. 'You look like a mummy!'

'Don't sneeze,' said Rondi. 'You'll blow your head off!'

They both laughed.

'Mh mhhh mhrhhmmm!' Jason said back to them. It was a very bad thing to say. He wasn't supposed to use words like that.

'You better not pull the tape off,' said Rondi. 'You might rip off your lips!'

They both laughed again.

Jason had never been more embarrassed in his whole life. His ears burned as he set to work on the arithmetic problems.

They were tough problems. Several times the pencil crashed against the tape, but the tape held firm.

Mrs Jewls was very proud of herself. Not only did the tape protect Myron's pencil, but Mrs Jewls also noticed that Jason was quieter than he'd ever been. I should tape all their mouths shut, she thought. Then they'd all be so nice and quiet.

It was such a good idea, she wondered why no other teacher had ever thought of it.

13

A GIGGLE BOX, A LEAKY TAP AND A FOGHORN

Every day after lunch Mrs Jewls read a story to the class.

Dana hated stories.

The last book Mrs Jewls had read was a story about a pig and spider. The pig was real cute and the spider was very wise.

Dana thought it was a horrible book. It made her laugh too much. Everyone else laughed too, but the problem was that Dana always kept laughing long after everyone else in the class had stopped. It was very embarrassing. And sometimes she broke out laughing at a part that wasn't even funny because she remembered something funny that had happened earlier.

John called her a giggle box.

That only made her laugh harder.

Once she broke up laughing in the middle of an arithmetic test because she remembered something funny the pig had said.

'There goes the giggle box,' said John.

She hated John.

But that wasn't the worst part of the book. In the end, the spider died.

Dana couldn't stop crying. And she thought it was so silly, too, because in real life she didn't even like spiders! She squashed them all the time.

John called her a leaky tap. 'Somebody better call a plumber to fix the leaky tap,' he said.

She laughed through her tears. She hated John.

Once in music, they had learned a song about a dragon. When the song begins the dragon is very brave, but then he loses his only friend, so he isn't brave any more. He just goes back to his cave, where he is sad and lonely for the rest of his life.

The song always made Dana cry. Every recess John and Joe would chase after her, singing it. She'd run across the playground with her hands over her ears and tears streaming down her face.

The bell rang. Lunch was over. Dana nervously walked up the stairs to Mrs Jewls's room. Mrs Jewls would start a new book today. She hoped it wouldn't be funny or sad. She hoped Mrs Jewls would read a boring story with no jokes.

When she got to class, John and Joe were standing by her desk waiting for her.

'Happy Birthday, Dana,' said John. He was holding a present. It was wrapped in green paper and had a pink bow.

'But it's not my birthday,' said Dana.

'Well, that's OK,' said John. 'You can have it anyway. Since I'm always teasing you.' He and Joe snickered.

Dana eagerly tore off the wrapping paper. Maybe John wasn't so bad after all, she thought.

It was a box of tissues.

John and Joe laughed hysterically.

'That's not funny!' said Dana. She raised her fist and started to chase after them.

Mrs Jewls rang her cowbell, and all the children settled quietly in their seats.

'We are ready to begin a new story,' said Mrs Jewls. She held up the book. 'It's called "Stinky."'

Dana laughed at the title, then quickly covered her mouth.

'It's about a cute and playful skunk,' said Mrs Jewls.

'Oh, no!' gasped Dana. She knew animal stories always made her cry. The animal's mother would get shot by human hunters. Or else humans would build a shopping centre and destroy the animal's home.

She hated humans. But she knew that was silly, because she was a human, and so were all her friends. The only human she really hated was John, and she didn't think he was even human!

Mrs Jewls read:

'It was such a beautiful day, Stinky and his mother went for a walk across the forest. "Hi, Stinky," said Charlie the chipmunk. "Hi, Charlie," said Stinky. "Come along, Stinky," called his mother. Stinky hurried after her. They came to a road. Suddenly Stinky heard a noise he had never heard before. It was very loud, like thunder. A car, driven by humans, was speeding towards him! "Look out!" shouted his mother. Stinky stopped in the middle of the road and stared at the onrushing car. He had never seen a car before. His mother pushed him out of the way just in time. He was safe, but unfortunately, the car ran over his mother. "Mama, Mama," he sobbed over and over again, but his mother didn't answer. She was dead.'

Dana cried.

'Uh-oh, there goes the leaky tap,' said John. He and Joe laughed.

Dana sniffled and wiped her eyes, but the tears wouldn't stop. She just kept thinking about poor Stinky. What would he do without his mother? she wondered. Maybe he could go live with Charlie the chipmunk, she hoped.

She pulled a tissue out of the box John had given her and loudly blew her nose.

'There goes the foghorn,' said John.

Dana laughed into her tissue. She blew her nose again, even louder.

'It must be a very foggy day,' said John.

The next day after lunch Dana hurried up the thirty flights of stairs before the bell rang, so she could talk to Mrs Jewls before class started.

'Yes, Dana?' said Mrs Jewls.

'Can I leave the room when you read today?' asked Dana.

'Why?' asked Mrs Jewls.

'Because I hate stories,' said Dana. 'They make me laugh and cry too much.'

'You don't hate stories, Dana,' Mrs Jewls told her. 'You love stories. I wish everybody laughed and cried as much as you.'

'Really?' asked Dana. She couldn't believe it. All this time she thought she hated stories when really she loved them. She was glad she really loved stories.

Suddenly she made a face. 'Oh, yuck!' she said.

'What is it?' asked Mrs Jewls.

'What if I really love John, too?'

14

CALVIN'S BIG DECISION

It was Calvin's birthday. His mother had made chocolate cupcakes with jelly beans on top. Mrs Jewls passed them out to the class.

'Hey, Dana,' said Leslie. 'I'll trade you my black jelly bean for your red one.'

'OK,' said Dana.

Everyone traded jelly beans. That was the most fun part of the party.

Bebe was very excited. 'Tell everybody what you're getting for your birthday, Calvin!' she said.

'I don't know,' Calvin mumbled as he stared at his yellow jelly bean.

'He's getting the best present!' said Bebe.

'What are you getting, Calvin?' asked Mrs Jewls.

Calvin frowned. 'I don't know!' he griped. 'I mean, I know what it is, but I don't know what it is.'

'Huh?' asked Jason.

'See, I usually get toys,' Calvin tried to explain. 'But they always break, or get lost, or something happens to them. But this year I'm getting something I'll never lose. I'll have it for the rest of my life.'

'What is it?' asked Terrence.

'A tattoo,' said Calvin.

'Oooh, how neat!' exclaimed Maurecia.

Everyone thought it was a great present.

'You're so lucky, Calvin,' said Rondi. 'I wish I could get a tattoo too! Instead I got a tutu.'

'I got a tutu too,' said Dana.

'My parents won't let me get a tattoo,' complained John.

'My parents wouldn't let me get one either,' said Calvin. 'Then, for my birthday, they said I could get one. But now I can't decide what to get. My dad's taking me to the tattoo parlour after school today! I just can't make up my mind.'

'Get a snake,' said Stephen.

'No, get an eagle,' said Deedee. 'They're the best!'

'A dead rat!' suggested Kathy.

'I just don't know,' said Calvin. 'I've never had to make such a tough decision. Nothing else I do matters very much. It's not like choosing jelly beans! If you pick the wrong colour jelly bean, big deal, you can always spit it out. But once you get a tattoo, you can't change your mind. You can't erase tattoos. Whatever I get I'll have for the rest of my life!'

'Get a naked lady,' said Jason.

Calvin shook his head. 'I just don't know. I just don't know.'

'Where are you going to put your tattoo?' asked Allison.

Calvin threw up his hands. 'I don't know!'

'You should put it on your arm,' said Myron. 'That's the best place for tattoos.'

'You're crazy, Myron,' said Todd. 'Put it on your chest, Calvin.'

'I know where you should put it,' said Dana. 'But I can't say.' She giggled like a maniac. Then she whispered it in Jenny's ear. Jenny giggled too.

All day everyone had lots of suggestions for Calvin. They told him what kind of tattoo he should get, and where he should put it. A rainbow on his forehead. A flower on his cheek. An anchor on his arm.

It was easy for the others to make suggestions. They wouldn't have to live with it for the rest of their lives.

'I just don't know,' Calvin repeated over and over again.

Bebe drew a lot of pictures for him, in case he wanted to choose one of those. She drew lions, tigers, buffaloes, and butterflies.

'If you like one, I can draw it on your skin for you,' said Bebe. 'Then the tattoo man can trace over it.'

'I just don't know,' muttered Calvin. 'I just don't know.'

After school Calvin's father picked him up and drove him to the tattoo parlour.

The next day when he walked into class, everybody stared at him. They couldn't see a tattoo.

'Did you get one?' asked Maurecia.

Calvin smiled. 'Yep,' he said.

'Where is it?' asked Jason.

Dana gasped. 'I know where!' she exclaimed.

She and Jenny giggled.

'Well, what'd you get?' asked Todd.

'It was a real tough decision,' said Calvin. 'I almost got a leopard fighting a snake. But then my dad told me to think about it. He said it was sort of like getting a second nose. You may think you want another nose, because that way if one nose gets stuffed up, you can breathe through the other nose. But then he asked me, "Calvin, do you really want two noses?"'

'Your father is very wise,' said Mrs Jewls.

Calvin nodded. 'That made me think,' he said. 'I decided I didn't want a snake and a leopard fighting on my body for the rest of my life. I suddenly knew exactly what I wanted.'

He pulled up his left trouser leg. There was a small tattoo just above his ankle.

Everyone crowded around to look at it.

'A potato!' exclaimed Leslie. 'How stupid!'

'That's the worst tattoo in the world!' said Mac.

They all thought it was a dumb tattoo.

'Anything is better than a potato!' said Jason.

'It's a pretty potato,' said Bebe, trying to be nice. 'I wish I could draw potatoes that good.' But even Bebe thought it was a dumb tattoo.

'I like potatoes,' said Calvin.

'I would hope so,' said Mrs Jewls.

Calvin could tell Mrs Jewls didn't like his tattoo either.

'I would have gotten an eagle,' said Deedee, 'soaring across the sky!'

'Not me,' said Terrence. 'I would have gotten a lion!'

'I would have gotten a kangaroo,' said Leslie.

All day everyone told Calvin what they would have got: a fire-breathing dragon, a lightning bolt, a creature from outer space.

None of them said they would have got a potato.

But Calvin knew better. He knew it was easy for his

friends to say what they would have got, because they really hadn't had to choose. He was the only one who really knew what it was like to pick a tattoo. Even Mrs Jewls didn't know that.

He looked at his potato. He smiled. It made him happy.

He was sure he had made the right choice.

At least he was pretty sure.

15

SHE'S BACK!

Deedee ran across the playground screaming.

At first Louis thought she was just having fun, but then he realised something was wrong. He hurried after her and grabbed her arm.

'Deedee, are you all right?' he asked.

She stared at him wide-eyed as she continued to scream.

Several other kids gathered around.

'What's wrong with Deedee?' asked Myron.

'I don't know,' said Louis.

Deedee hiccuped three times, then gasped, 'I saw her!'

'Who?' asked Louis.

Deedee didn't answer – she just stared right through him.

But everyone else knew whom Deedee had seen. Most of them had seen her too, during the last two weeks.

'Where was she?' asked Todd.

'On the monkey bars,' said Deedee, still trembling and breathing hard.

'I was hanging upside down, and suddenly she was hanging upside down right next to me!'

'Did she wiggle her ears?' asked Jenny.

'Only one,' said Deedee. 'I jumped off and ran away before she could wiggle the other one.'

'That's good,' said Rondi.

'Who is she?' asked Louis. 'A hippopotamus?'

'No!' said Myron with a laugh. 'Why do you say that?'

'Because when a hippopotamus gets mad, it wiggles its ears.'

'She's worse than a hippopotamus,' said Allison.

'I saw her last week, at the water fountain,' said Todd. 'I bent down to get a drink, and then there she was, drinking at the tap next to me.'

'I saw her on the stairs,' said Rondi. 'I was going up the stairs, and she went right past me, sliding down on the banister.'

'Who?' asked Louis.

'Mrs Gorf!' said Deedee. Just saying the name sent a shiver of fear through her body.

'Oh, your old teacher,' said Louis with a shrug. 'Is she back? I always wondered what happened to her.'

The children looked at each other. Mrs Gorf was the teacher they had had before Mrs Jewls took over. They had never told anyone how they had got rid of her. They especially couldn't tell Louis.

She was the meanest teacher in the history of Wayside School. Of course there are other teachers at other schools who are meaner.

Louis looked towards the monkey bars. 'I don't see her,' he said.

'Well, she was there,' Deedee insisted. 'I saw her!'

'You just imagined you saw her, Deedee,' said Louis. 'If you hate somebody, or if you love somebody, you often think you see that person when she isn't there. It's very common. It's just like Mrs Drazil.'

'Who's Mrs Drazil?' asked Todd.

'She was the worst teacher I ever had,' said Louis. He shivered just thinking about her. 'She was my teacher when I was your age. I sometimes think I see her, too. And I still have nightmares about her.'

'Was she mean?' asked Rondi.

'She was *horrible!*' said Louis. 'Every morning she used to check our fingernails. If they were dirty, she'd tell the whole class. "Louis has dirty fingernails this morning," she'd say in a really nasty voice. And if you talked in class, she would pick up the wastepaper basket and put it over your head. You had to leave it on your head until the bell rang.'

'Did she ever put it over your head?' asked Todd.

'Lots of times,' said Louis.

Everybody laughed.

'It wasn't funny,' said Louis. 'My mother always knew when I got in trouble, because I'd have bits of trash stuck in my hair.'

'Did it get stuck in your moustache, too?' asked Rondi.

'Louis didn't have a moustache when he was our age!' said Allison. 'Did you, Louis?' she asked.

Suddenly, Louis screamed.

Everyone stared at him.

'She's back!' he shouted, as he shook with fear. Then he slapped himself in the face. 'Excuse me,' he said. 'Sorry. For a second I thought I saw Mrs Drazil.'

He turned to Deedee. 'C'mon, let's go to the monkey bars.'

'No!' declared Deedee. 'I'm not going back. I'm never getting on the monkey bars again!'

Louis took hold of her hand. 'Mrs Gorf isn't there,' he said. 'You just imagined her.'

They headed to the monkey bars. No one else dared to follow.

'If she starts to wiggle her ears, run away as fast as you can,' warned Deedee. She held tightly on to Louis's hand.

When they reached the monkey bars, no one was there. 'Where were you when you saw her?' Louis asked.

'I was hanging upside down over there,' said Deedee, pointing.

'OK, go hang upside down,' said Louis.

'No!' exclaimed Deedee.

'Don't worry, I'll be right here in case anything happens.'

It had rained during the night, so the sand under the monkey bars was wet and somewhat hard.

Deedee walked across the sand and pulled herself up on the bar. She hooked her legs over, then hung from her knees.

'Well, do you see her?' Louis asked.

'No, it's safe now,' said Deedee. 'Thanks, Louis. I guess you're right. I must have seen my shadow or something.'

Deedee pulled herself right side up, then hopped down from the monkey bars. She and Louis walked away hand in hand. She held Louis's hand not because she was scared but because she liked him.

'Mrs Drazil sounds almost as bad as Mrs Gorf,' said Deedee.

'She was,' said Louis. 'She once made me put gum on my nose, because I was chewing it in class.'

'How can you chew your nose?' asked Deedee.

Behind them, Deedee's footprints could be seen in the wet sand under the monkey bars. There was also another set of footprints, made by a person who had much bigger feet.

16

LOVE AND A DEAD RAT

Dameon was in love with one of the girls in his class. Can you guess which one?

He thought about her all the time.

Myron threw a red ball to Dameon. It bounced off his face.

'Huh?' said Dameon.

'Why didn't you catch the ball?' asked Myron.

'What ball?' asked Dameon.

'The one that hit you in the face,' said Myron.

'Did a ball hit me in the face?' asked Dameon.

'Yes,' said Myron.

'Oh, good,' said Dameon. 'I was wondering why my nose hurt.'

He had been thinking about the girl he loved.

He was in love with Mrs Jewls.

That was why he was always doing things for her, like passing out papers. He thought she was very pretty and nice. He thought she was smart, too. In fact, he thought she was one of the smartest people in the class.

After recess he hurried back up the stairs.

'Hello, Dameon,' said Mrs Jewls.

'Hello, Mrs Jewls,' he said.

'You're always the first one here, aren't you?' asked Mrs Jewls.

Dameon blushed and shrugged his shoulders. 'Do you need any papers passed out or anything?' he asked.

'It's so nice of you to ask,' said Mrs Jewls.

'I think you're nice too,' said Dameon.

Mrs Jewls gave him a stack of workbooks to hand out. Then she gave him a Tootsie Roll Pop from the coffee can on her desk for being so helpful. 'But don't eat it until after lunch,' she said.

'I won't,' he assured her.

He ate lunch with Myron and D.J. He saved his Tootsie Roll Pop for last.

Joy and Maurecia came up behind him.

'Hi, Dameon,' said Joy. 'How's your *girlfriend?*'

'What?' asked Dameon. He turned red. 'Who are you talking about? I don't have a girlfriend!'

'You're in love with Mrs Jewls!' accused Maurecia.

'You better watch out,' said Joy. 'Mister Jewls might come after you.'

The two girls laughed.

'I don't know what you're talking about,' said Dameon. 'I'm not in love with Mrs Jewls!' He looked to his friends for support.

Myron shrugged.

D.J. smiled.

'Prove it!' said Joy. 'Prove you're not in love with her.'

'That's stupid,' said Dameon. 'How can I prove I'm not in love with Mrs Jewls?'

'Give her this,' said Joy. She handed Dameon a paper bag.

'Your lunch?' asked Dameon.

'Look inside,' said Maurecia.

Inside the paper bag was a dead rat.

Dameon knew Mrs Jewls hated dead rats more than anything in the world.

'Put it in her desk,' said Joy.

'If you don't, it means you love her,' said Maurecia.

'I'm not in love with her,' said Dameon.

'Prove it,' said Joy.

'OK, I will!' said Dameon.

The girls left.

'You don't have to put the dead rat in her desk,' said D.J.

'We don't care,' said Myron.

'You think I'm in love with her too, don't you?' asked Dameon.

Myron shrugged.

D.J. smiled.

'Some friends you are!' said Dameon. 'I'll show you!'

After lunch he was the first one back in class. He carried Joy's paper bag.

'Hello, Dameon,' said Mrs Jewls. 'Did you have a nice lunch?'

'It was all right,' he muttered.

'Oh, would you mind getting the construction paper from the closet and putting it on my desk?' asked Mrs Jewls. 'Thank you.'

Dameon went to the closet and got the construction paper. He put it on her desk. Then, when she wasn't looking he opened her desk drawer and dumped the dead rat into it. He shut the drawer.

'Thank you, Dameon,' said Mrs Jewls. 'You're always so helpful. It's such a pleasure to have you in my class.'

Dameon felt awful.

Mrs Jewls read a story to the class.

Dameon couldn't pay attention. He kept wondering when she'd open her drawer.

After the story they had art. Everyone was supposed to make snowflakes.

Dameon folded his piece of construction paper in half.

Mrs Jewls screamed.

'What's wrong, Mrs Jewls?' asked Joy.

'Somebody put a dead rat in my desk,' said Mrs Jewls.

'I did!' declared Dameon.

'Dameon?' Mrs Jewls said with great surprise. 'Why?'

'Because I hate you!' said Dameon. 'You're always making me do things for you.'

'Oh, I see,' said Mrs Jewls.

'Should I write my name on the board under DISCIPLINE?' he asked.

'No, that won't be necessary,' said Mrs Jewls.

That made him feel even worse. Why did I have to prove myself to Joy? he wondered. I don't like Joy. I like Mrs Jewls. He felt rotten.

When the bell rang, Dameon waited for all the other kids to leave. Then he walked to Mrs Jewls's desk.

She was grading papers. 'Yes, Dameon?'

'Do you want me to erase the board for you?' he asked.

'That's all right,' said Mrs Jewls. 'I'll do it myself.'

Dameon sadly walked out of the room and down the stairs. When he reached the bottom, he turned and ran all the way back up to Mrs Jewls's room.

She was just putting on her coat.

'I love you, Mrs Jewls!' Dameon declared. 'I'm sorry I put the dead rat in your desk. I did it because I didn't want everyone to know I loved you. I'm sorry.'

'I love you, too, Dameon,' said Mrs Jewls.

'You do? But what about Mister Jewls?'

'Just because I love Mister Jewls, it doesn't mean I can't also love you. Love is different from most things.' She picked up a piece of chalk. 'If I gave my piece of chalk to someone, then I wouldn't have it any more. But when I give my love to someone, I end up with more love than I started with. The more love you give away, the more you have left.'

Dameon smiled. 'I love you, Mrs Jewls,' he said. He felt his heart fill up with more love.

'I love you, Dameon,' said Mrs Jewls.

'This is getting disgusting!' said the dead rat. It climbed out of Mrs Jewls's desk and walked out of the room.

17

WHAT?

It was purple.

So Jenny read the story backwards. When she finished, she threw up.

'OK,' said Jenny.

'So read the story backwards,' suggested Mrs Jewls. 'That way the beginning will be a surprise.'

'But I already know how the story ends!' Jenny complained. 'I only like stories with surprise endings.'

'Good point,' said Mrs Jewls. 'Here, you can read the story yourself. It's very funny.' She gave the book to Jenny.

'All I heard was the last sentence,' said Jenny. 'It isn't funny unless you know what happened first.'

'Why aren't you laughing, Jenny?' asked Mrs Jewls. 'Didn't you think it was a funny story?'

That made Dana laugh harder.

'There goes the giggle box,' said Myron.

Everybody laughed, except for Jenny. Dana laughed hysterically.

Mrs Jewls looked back at the story she had been reading before Jenny's interruption. There was only one sentence left for her to read. She read it to the class.

Jenny made a face. She could still taste the awful stuff.

'And next time you'll drink your prune juice more quickly,' said Mrs Jewls.

Jenny sat down.

Mrs Jewls waited for Jenny to sit down.

Jenny wrote her name on the blackboard under the word DISCIPLINE.

'Well, that's no excuse,' said Mrs Jewls. 'Now go write your name on the blackboard under the word DISCIPLINE.'

'I couldn't leave the table until I finished it,' explained Jenny. 'And then I missed the bus.'

'What does prune juice have to do with anything?' asked Mrs Jewls.

'Because I hate prune juice!' Jenny griped.

'Why are you late?' asked Mrs Jewls.

'I can't hear you,' said Jenny. 'I better take off my

helmet.' She took off her helmet.

'Take off your helmet,' said Mrs Jewls.

'What?' asked Jenny.

'Why are you late?' asked Mrs Jewls.

Jenny caught her breath. 'What?' she asked. She couldn't hear too well because she was still wearing the motorcycle helmet.

Mrs Jewls looked up from the story she had been reading to the class. 'You're late,' she said.

She hopped off the bike in front of Wayside School and charged up the stairs. Her stomach was still going up and down as she opened the door to Mrs Jewls's room.

She put on her helmet; then her father drove her to school on the back of his motorcycle. It was a very bumpy ride.

'Put on your helmet,' said her father. 'I'll drive you to school on the back of my motorcycle.'

'I missed the bus,' Jenny grumbled.

'What are you doing home?' asked her mother.

She finally got it all down, then hurried as fast as she could to the bus stop. When she got there, the bus was just pulling away. She sighed, then turned around and ran all the way back home.

Her mother wouldn't let her leave the breakfast table until she finished her prune juice. It took her forever. She hated prune juice more than anything in the world.

One day Jenny was late for school.

18

THE SUBSTITUTE

Benjamin couldn't take it any longer. Today was the day he would finally tell Mrs Jewls his real name.

So what if nobody likes me? he thought. So what if I stop getting high marks?

'Hi, Mark,' said Jason.

'Hi, Mark,' said Stephen.

'Hi, hi,' he glumly replied, then started up the stairs.

'Hi, Mark,' said Bebe as he took his seat next to her. 'Guess what? We have a substitute!'

'Yahoooo!' shouted Maurecia.

Everyone in Mrs Jewls's class loved it when they had substitute teachers. They loved playing mean and horrible tricks on them.

Benjamin frowned. He finally had the courage to tell Mrs Jewls his real name. 'Rats!' he said.

'That's a good idea!' said Terrence. 'We'll put dead rats in her desk!'

'Let's trick her into going outside,' said Joy, 'then lock her out of the room.'

'But what if she tells Mr Kidswatter?' asked Eric Fry.

'So what?' said Joy. 'She'll have to go all the way down to the office, and then all the way back up. By then we'll unlock the door. Mr Kidswatter will think she's bonkers!'

Benjamin looked at the substitute teacher sitting at Mrs Jewls's desk. She looked like a nice lady. She wore tiny spectacles and had long grey hair tied in a ponytail. He felt sorry for her, and he felt sorry for himself. I was going to tell Mrs Jewls my name, he thought. I really was!

The substitute stood up and walked to the centre of the room. 'Good morning,' she said. 'My name is Mrs Franklin.'

Nobody said 'Good morning' back to her.

Calvin handed Benjamin a note: *At ten o'clock drop your book on the floor. Pass it on.*

Benjamin read it, then passed it on to Todd.

'OK, who can tell me what page we're on?' asked Mrs Franklin.

'Page seventeen,' called Myron.

'A hundred and twelve,' said Maurecia.

'Ninety-eight,' said Eric Ovens.

'Three thousand,' said Joe.

Mrs Franklin smiled. 'I guess we'll have to study all those pages,' she said.

Benjamin raised his hand.

'Yes, the handsome young man in the red shirt,' said the substitute.

He told her the correct page. 'We're on page one hundred and two,' he said.

'Thank you,' said the substitute. 'And what is your name, please?'

Benjamin thought a moment. He looked around the room, then boldly told the truth. 'My name is Benjamin!' he stated proudly.

Several kids snickered.

'Thank you, Benjamin,' said the substitute. There were more snickers.

'You're welcome,' said Benjamin. He felt good, even if the other kids were laughing at him.

Mrs Franklin asked a question from page 102.

Jason answered it correctly.

'Very good,' said the substitute. 'And what is your name, please?'

Jason looked around. 'Benjamin!' he asserted.

Half the class giggled.

'Thank you, Benjamin,' said Mrs Franklin.

The other half giggled.

Dana answered the next question.

'And what's your name?' Mrs Franklin asked Dana.

'Benjamin!' Dana blurted, then fell giggling on to the floor.

'Thank you, Benjamin,' said the substitute.

Everyone was hysterical.

'My, it is certainly a pleasure to teach such happy students,' said the substitute. 'Who knows the answer to question four?'

They all raised their hands. They all wanted to tell the substitute their names were Benjamin.

They were having so much fun, they forgot to drop their books at ten o'clock.

At recess everyone congratulated Benjamin on his great trick.

'You're a genius, Mark,' said Todd.

'Benjamin is such a funny name,' said Jason. 'How'd you ever think of it?'

'But my name really is Benjamin,' said Benjamin.

'So is mine,' said Stephen.

'Mine too,' said Leslie.

They all laughed.

'Do you think she really believes we're all named Benjamin?' asked Eric Ovens.

'Probably,' said Joy. 'She's so stupid!'

'If she thought we were lying, she would have gotten mad,' said Eric Bacon.

The bell rang, and they all hurried back to class. After recess was social studies.

'Who would like to read?' asked Mrs Franklin. Every hand went up.

'OK, Benjamin,' said Mrs Franklin as she pointed at Dana.

Everyone laughed.

Dana giggled a few seconds, then got control of herself and read from the book.

'Thank you, Benjamin,' said the substitute when Dana finished reading. 'OK, Benjamin, you may read next,' she said, pointing at Terrence.

Everyone laughed.

It was the first time all year Terrence had volunteered to read.

All day, everyone paid very close attention. They all wanted the teacher to call on them. Because as funny as it was when Mrs Franklin called somebody else Benjamin, it was even funnier when she called you Benjamin.

So everyone worked hard and listened closely. As a result, they learned more from the substitute in a day than they usually learned from Mrs Jewls in a month.

When the final bell rang, everyone crowded around her desk.

'Are you coming back tomorrow, Mrs Franklin?' asked Eric Bacon.

'Please, Mrs Franklin, say you will,' pleaded Kathy.

'You're the best substitute teacher we've ever had!' said Jason.

The substitute smiled. 'School is over,' she said. 'You don't have to call me Mrs Franklin any more. That sounds so formal. Since we're friends now, you may call me by my first name.'

'What is your first name?' asked Maurecia.

The substitute gathered up her things and put them in a straw bag. 'Benjamin,' she said, then walked out of the room.

Everyone stared silently after her.

'Do you think that's really her name?' asked Joy.

19

A BAD CASE OF THE SILLIES

Allison started up the stairs five minutes before the bell rang for school to start. The stairs were completely empty. Allison liked it that way. When the bell rang, the stairs would be crammed with a thousand screaming kids scurrying to their rooms, but now it was nice and peaceful.

She walked up past the eighteenth storey and towards the twentieth. There was no nineteenth storey in Wayside School. Miss Zarves taught the class on the nineteenth storey. There was no Miss Zarves.

Allison didn't understand it. If there was no nineteenth storey, then wasn't her class really on the twenty-ninth?

Suddenly she heard footsteps charging up behind her. She turned around to see Ron and Deedee racing.

She leaned against the wall to get out of their way, but Deedee stamped on her foot; then Ron's elbow jammed her in the stomach.

'Umph!' she grunted, as she fell and rolled down three steps.

Deedee and Ron didn't even stop to say they were sorry.

Allison slowly stood up. Fortunately she wasn't hurt, but her windbreaker was torn.

She thought Ron and Deedee were silly. They race up the stairs, and then when they get to Mrs Jewls's room they're too pooped to learn anything.

Allison thought all the kids in Mrs Jewls's class were silly, even Rondi, and Rondi was her best friend. Then there was Jason, who was always pestering her. That was because Jason hated her. Or else he loved her. Allison wasn't sure which.

When she got to class, Deedee and Ron were sitting with their heads flat on their desks and their tongues hanging out.

'You could have said you were sorry,' Allison said as she walked past them. She sat up straight in her chair, folded her hands on her desk, and waited as everyone else wandered in.

Jason entered the room carrying a glass bowl with a goldfish swimming inside it. 'Look what I brought!' he said.

'What's the name of your goldfish?' asked Mrs Jewls.

'Shark!' said Jason.

Everyone laughed. Allison rolled her eyes.

'It makes him feel important,' Jason explained. 'Where should I put him?'

'How about on top of the coat closet?' suggested Mrs Jewls.

Jason had to stand on a chair on his tiptoes. He held the bowl at the very bottom as he tried to nudge it over the edge of the closet.

Suddenly the chair toppled over. 'Aaaaaahh-gulp!' yelled Jason as he fell on the floor. He was holding the bowl upside down above his wet face.

Mrs Jewls hurried to the back of the room. 'Quick, somebody fill the bowl with water,' she said. 'Where's Shark?'

Jason made a face. 'I swallowed him.'

The class went crazy.

What a show-off, thought Allison.

Mrs Jewls rang her cowbell and told everyone to settle down. 'You have a bad case of the sillies this morning,' she said.

She took roll. 'Who's absent?' she asked.

'Allison,' said Rondi.

111

'Very funny, Rondi,' said Allison.

'Anybody besides Allison?' asked Mrs Jewls.

'I'm here, Mrs Jewls,' said Allison. She sat behind Eric Fry, so she thought Mrs Jewls couldn't see her. Eric Fry was the biggest kid in the class.

'Just Allison,' said Mrs Jewls. She marked it on her green roll card. 'Dameon, will you please take the roll card to the office.'

Allison stood up. 'I'm not absent,' she said.

Dameon took the roll card and walked out the door.

'Mrs Jewls, did you just mark me absent?' asked Allison.

Mrs Jewls didn't answer her.

Allison marched to her desk. 'Mrs Jewls, did you mark me absent?' she asked again.

Mrs Jewls looked up. 'Terrence, what are you whispering about?'

'Nothing,' mumbled Terrence.

'If you can say it to Jenny, you can say it to me,' said Mrs Jewls.

'Get off my case, Buzzard Face!' said Terrence.

'Terrence!' exclaimed Mrs Jewls. 'Go write your name on the blackboard under the word DISCIPLINE.'

'But that's what I said to Jenny,' Terrence protested.

'Mrs Jewls, what about me?' Allison demanded.

Mrs Jewls ignored her.

Allison screamed as loud as she could.

Mrs Jewls didn't hear her.

Allison faced the class. 'Can't anybody see me?' she asked.

Nobody answered her.

'Rondi?' shouted Allison. 'Dana? Jason?

'This isn't funny,' said Allison. 'I know you're all just pretending.' She stood right in front of Jason, leaned over his desk, and stared him straight in the eye. 'I know you can see me,' she said. 'You're trying not to laugh.'

He stared right through her.

She stuck out her tongue at him.

He leaned forward, causing Allison's tongue to lick his nose.

'Yuck!' she exclaimed, then wiped her tongue on her sleeve.

Mrs Jewls began the morning lesson.

'Have you gone crazy?' shouted Allison. She ran out of the room and down to the class on the twenty-ninth storey. 'Come quick,' she said. 'There's something wrong with Mrs Jewls's class.'

No one heard her.

She slammed the door, then continued down the stairs to the class on the twenty-eighth floor. No one saw her there, either.

Tears streamed down her cheeks. Is the whole school playing a joke on me? she wondered. 'It's not funny!' she shouted as loud as she could.

She continued down the stairs, screaming anything that came to her head, hoping that someone, somewhere, would notice her.

'Fish for sale! Fresh fish! Fat fish! Get your fresh, fat fish!'

A tall, skinny lady with very short hair stepped out of one of the classrooms. 'Shh!' she whispered. 'This is a school, not a fish market!'

'You can hear me?' asked Allison. She was so happy, she wanted to hug her.

'Yes, I can hear you,' the woman said sternly. 'My whole class can hear you. You're making it impossible for us to get any work done.'

'I'm sorry,' said Allison. 'But something's wrong in Mrs Jewls's class.'

'You'd better come in here,' said the teacher.

Allison followed the teacher into her classroom.

'What's your name?' the teacher asked her.

'Allison.'

'Boys and girls, this is Allison,' the teacher announced to her students. 'She'll be joining our class.'

'What?' said Allison. 'But –'

'My name is Miss Zarves,' said the teacher. 'Welcome to the nineteenth storey.'

19

A WONDERFUL TEACHER

Allison was still on the nineteenth storey.

The desks were arranged in clusters of four. Allison sat at a cluster with a girl named Virginia, a boy named Nick, and a boy named Ray.

But Virginia looked old enough to be her mother. And Nick looked like he should be in high school. Ray was a couple of years younger than Allison.

'Miss Zarves is a wonderful teacher,' said Virginia in a singsong voice. 'She's the nicest teacher I ever had.'

'She's the *only* teacher you ever had,' said Nick.

'So? She's still nice,' said Virginia. 'I've always gotten all A's.'

'Aren't you a little old to be going to school?' Allison asked her.

'You're never too old to learn,' said Virginia.

'No one ever leaves Miss Zarves's class,' said Nick. 'How long have you been here, Virginia?'

Virginia thought a moment. 'Thirty-two wonderful years.'

'I've been here nine years,' said Nick.

'But she always gives us good grades,' said Virginia.

'That's true,' Nick agreed. 'I've gotten all A's since I've been here too.'

'Me too,' said Ray. 'And sometimes I answer all the problems wrong on purpose!'

'Where were you before you came here?' Allison asked him.

'I went to, um, I was ...' Ray shook his head. 'That's funny – I don't remember.'

'I don't remember where I came from either,' said Virginia.

'Well, I do!' said Allison. 'I was in ...' But suddenly she couldn't remember either. Then it came to her. 'Mrs Jewls's class! And Rondi was in the class, and Jason, and Dana, and Todd ...'

She named every member of the class, including all three Erics. She didn't want to forget where she came from. If I forget where I came from, I might never get back, she thought.

'Did you say there was a girl named Bebe Gunn?' asked Ray.

'Yes,' said Allison. 'Bebe's a very good artist.'

'My last name is Gunn, too,' said Ray. 'I wonder if we're related.'

'Ray, no talking please,' said Miss Zarves. 'Now, everyone please take out a pencil and some paper. I want you to write all the numbers from zero to a million in alphabetical order.'

'From zero to a million?' asked Allison. She couldn't believe it.

'Don't worry,' said Virginia. 'If you run out of paper, Miss Zarves has more in the closet.'

Allison stared at her in horror. 'But it will take over a hundred years,' she said.

'So?' asked Virginia. 'What's your hurry?'

Allison started to work. It was bad enough having to write down all the numbers from zero to a million, but she couldn't imagine how she'd ever put them in alphabetical order.

One came before two.

Three came after one, but before two.

Four came before one.

Five came before four.

Six came after one, but before three.

'Don't worry,' said Virginia. 'Even if you miss a few, Miss Zarves will give you an A when you finish.'

Seven came after one and before six.

Eight came first. Allison couldn't think of any number that would come before eight, so she wrote it down. She also knew zero would come last, if she ever got that far. By then she'd be older than Virginia.

I'll talk to Louis at recess, she thought. He'll save me.

'When's recess?' she asked.

'There is no recess,' said Ray. 'We're not allowed out of the classroom.'

'What about if you have to go to the bathroom?'

'What's a bathroom?' asked Virginia.

'We don't eat, either,' said Nick. 'We just work all the time.'

'But we never have homework,' Virginia said cheerfully.

'That's because we never go home,' said Nick. 'We get a two-minute break every eleven hours.'

'But don't worry,' said Virginia. 'Miss Zarves always gives us good grades.'

Miss Zarves walked around the room checking everybody's work. 'Excellent, Ray!' she said. 'Very good, Virginia. You're doing wonderfully, Allison. You get an A for the day.'

Big deal! thought Allison. She had to figure out some way out of there. It was clear that Virginia, Nick, and Ray were all too far gone to help her.

'Are there any other new kids in the class?' she asked.

'Ben's new,' said Nick. He pointed Ben out to her.

Ben appeared to be about Allison's age. She was glad about that. When the two-minute break came, she went over and talked to him.

'Are you Ben?' she asked.

'No,' he said.

'Oh,' said Allison. 'I was looking for Ben.'

'That's me,' said the boy.

'But you just said –'

'My name's Mark Miller,' said the boy. 'But for some reason everybody calls me Benjamin Nushmutt.'

'There's a Mark Miller in my class!' exclaimed Allison.

'I know, that's me,' said Mark. 'I'm Mark Miller.'

'No, I mean my other class,' said Allison.

'What other class?'

Allison thought a moment. 'I don't remember …' she said.

After putting numbers in alphabetical order for eleven hours, her brain had turned into spaghetti.

'Time's up,' said Miss Zarves. 'Everyone back to work.'

19

FOREVER IS NEVER

Allison was still stuck on the nineteenth storey.

Fourteen two-minute breaks had passed.

'It's dictionary time,' said Miss Zarves.

Everybody got out a dictionary. Allison found a dictionary in her desk, too.

'What are we supposed to do with it?' she asked.

'Memorise it,' said Nick.

'But that's impossible!' said Allison.

'No, it's easy,' Virginia assured her. 'You memorise one word at a time, until you get a whole page. Then you go on to the next page.'

'How many words have you memorised?' asked Allison.

'I'm almost finished with the B's,' Virginia said proudly. 'And I've only been doing it for thirty-two years!'

Allison opened her dictionary. *Mrs Jewls's class!* she suddenly remembered. She sighed with relief. For the last six days she'd been trying to remember where she came from.

In her mind she went through everybody in her former class. She didn't want to forget again. As she thought about each person, tears filled her eyes. She missed them very much. Even Jason. They were all so wonderful in their own special ways.

When the two-minute break came, she talked to Mark again. He was the only person in the class who still seemed to have a brain.

'How did we get here?' she asked.

'Maybe we're dead,' said Mark. 'Maybe we died and went to —'

'This isn't Heaven!' said Allison.

'That wasn't what I was going to say,' said Mark.

Allison felt a chill run up her spine. She looked at Miss Zarves. Miss Zarves smiled back at her.

'But she seems so nice,' said Allison. 'Could someone as nice as her really be the devil?'

'I don't know,' said Mark. 'She always gives good grades.'

'What would happen if we didn't do our work?' asked Allison.

'We have to do our work,' said Mark.

'Why?' asked Allison. 'What's Miss Zarves going to do to us – keep us after school?'

'I don't know,' said Mark. 'Teachers can always find new ways to punish you. They're experts at it.'

'Your two minutes are up, boys and girls,' announced Miss Zarves. 'Everyone back to work.'

Allison returned to her seat. She tried to figure it all out, but she had so much busy work to do, she didn't have time to think.

That's her plan! Allison suddenly realised. She shivered as it all came together for her. Miss Zarves assigns us lots of busy work so we don't have time to think. She makes us memorise stupid things so that we don't think about the important things. And then she gives us good grades to keep us happy.

Miss Zarves walked around the room. 'Very good, Virginia,' she said. 'You are doing so well. Excellent, Ray! Good job, Nick.' She stopped when she got to Allison. 'Allison, why aren't you working?'

Allison looked at her. She knew Mark was right. Teachers are experts at finding ways to punish you. And if Miss Zarves was the devil, who knew what she might have up her sleeve? Still, Allison had to take a chance. If she wanted to get back to Mrs Jewls's class, she had to act as if she were in Mrs Jewls's class.

She took off her shoes and socks, sat on the floor, and sucked her toes.

'Allison, what are you doing?' asked Miss Zarves.

Allison took her toe out of her mouth. 'Get off my case, Buzzard Face,' she said.

Miss Zarves was furious. 'Return to your desk, young lady!' she ordered.

Allison returned to her desk. But instead of sitting at it, she climbed on top of it and sang a song.

'I got one sock!
    Lookin' for the other.
One sock!
    Lookin' for its brother.
When I find that sock!
    I'll tell you what I'll do.
I'll put it on my foot,
    and I'll stick it in my shoe!'

Mark Miller smiled at her and silently clapped his hands. Everyone else looked at her like she was crazy.

'Your socks are on the floor, next to your shoes,' Miss Zarves said coldly. 'I'll give you ten seconds to put them on your feet. Ten … nine … eight … seven …'

Allison climbed down from her desk. She picked up her socks and put them on her ears. 'How's this?' she asked.

'Six … five … four …'

'Albert Einstein didn't wear socks,' said Allison. 'Why should I?'

'Three … two …'

Allison closed her eyes.

'One!'

She felt something slam down on her foot. Something else jammed into her stomach. 'Umph!' she grunted as she fell and rolled down three steps.

'Are you all right?' asked Deedee.

'Huh?' said Allison. She was on the stairs, somewhere between the eighteenth and twentieth storeys.

'Sorry,' said Ron. 'I didn't see you. Deedee and I were racing up the stairs, and then you suddenly appeared.'

'You knocked off her shoes and socks!' exclaimed Deedee.

'Oh, I ripped your windbreaker, too,' said Ron. 'I'm sorry.'

'That's OK,' said Allison. She picked up her shoes and socks. 'Race you up the stairs!'

All three ran up to Mrs Jewls's room. When they got there, they were so pooped, they sat with their heads flat on their desks and their tongues hanging out.

'Hi, Allison,' said Rondi.

Allison raised her head. 'Hi, Rondi,' she said happily. 'What did I miss while I was absent?'

'When were you absent?' asked Rondi. 'Hey, how come you're not wearing your shoes and socks?'

Allison hung her socks from her ears. 'What do you think?' she asked. 'It's the new look!'

Rondi laughed.

'Allison,' said Mrs Jewls, 'you seem to have a bad case of the sillies this morning.'

Allison giggled.

Jason entered the room carrying a glass bowl with a goldfish swimming inside it. 'Look what I brought!' he said.

'What's the name of your goldfish?' asked Mrs Jewls.

'Shark!' said Jason.

Everyone laughed.

'It makes him feel important,' Jason explained. 'Where should I put him?'

'How about on top of the coat closet?' suggested Mrs Jewls.

Jason had to stand on a chair on his tiptoes. He held the bowl at the very bottom as he tried to nudge it over the edge of the closet.

Allison turned around to watch. She didn't want to miss this!

20, 21 & 22
ERIC, ERIC AND ERIC

Mr Kidswatter's voice crackled over the loudspeaker. 'MRS JEWLS, SEND ERIC TO MY OFFICE, AT ONCE!' He sounded mad.

Mrs Jewls was confused. 'When did we get a loud-speaker?' she asked.

'Louis put it in yesterday,' said Jenny.

Mrs Jewls was still confused. There were three Erics in her class. She didn't know which one Mr Kidswatter meant.

Eric Fry was fat, but not short.

Eric Bacon was short, but not fat.

Eric Ovens was short and fat.

Mrs Jewls chose the biggest Eric. 'Eric Fry, Mr Kidswatter wants to see you.'

Eric Fry trembled as he slowly stood up.

The other two Erics smiled.

The principal's office was on the first floor. It's not fair, Eric thought as he headed down to his doom. Anytime any Eric does something wrong, I'm the one who gets in trouble.

He stood in front of the principal's door. His heart beat very fast. He took a couple of breaths, then knocked lightly.

'Enter!' boomed Mr Kidswatter.

Eric turned the doorknob. He took one step inside, then stood with his back against the wall, as far away from Mr Kidswatter as he could get.

Mr Kidswatter sat behind an enormous desk. He wore mirrored sunglasses so Eric couldn't tell where he was looking. 'Sit down, Eric,' he said.

Eric moved to the small metal chair in front of the desk. A bare light bulb hung above his head.

Mr Kidswatter cracked his knuckles. 'We can do this the easy way, or we can do this the hard way,' he said. 'It's your choice.'

'I don't know what you're talking about,' said Eric. 'I didn't do anything.'

'So it's the hard way, is it?' asked Mr Kidswatter. 'Very well. You'll talk. One way or another, you'll tell me everything I want to know.'

'But —'

Mr Kidswatter pounded his fist on his desk. 'When was the last time you sharpened your pencil?'

Eric tried to remember, but he was too nervous to think. 'Um, wait, let me think,' he stammered. 'We had a spelling test on Friday, but I borrowed –'

'Where were you yesterday afternoon, at a quarter past twelve?' asked Mr Kidswatter.

'Yesterday?' asked Eric. 'I was here, at Wayside School. I remember I ate lunch and then I played kickball.'

Mr Kidswatter smiled. 'Do you kick with your left foot?' he asked.

'No, I'm right-footed,' said Eric Fry.

'Hmph!' grumbled Mr Kidswatter. 'Have you ever gotten your hair cut at Charley's Barber Shop?'

'Yes,' said Eric. 'Two weeks ago.'

'Aha!' said Mr Kidswatter. 'So you admit it! Do you know what a Mugworm Griblick is?'

Eric Fry turned pale. 'No, please!' he begged. 'I didn't do it! I'm innocent! You've got the wrong Eric. There are two other Erics in my class.'

Mr Kidswatter scowled. 'So that's the way you're going to play it, is it? Well, that's fine with me. I've got all the time in the world.'

He flicked on the microphone. 'MRS JEWLS! SEND ME ANOTHER ERIC!'

Twenty-nine floors above them, Mrs Jewls looked at the two remaining Erics.

'OK, Eric Ovens,' she said.

Eric Ovens shivered. His eyes filled with tears.

Why me? he asked himself over and over again as he walked down the stairs. It's my parents' fault! Why did they have to name me Eric? Why couldn't they name me Osgood?

He tapped on the door to the principal's office.

'Come in!' bellowed Mr Kidswatter.

Eric Ovens gulped, then walked inside. He sat in the little chair in front of Mr Kidswatter's enormous desk.

Eric Fry was nowhere to be seen.

'Wh-what ha-happened to Eric Fry?' he asked.

'I'll ask the questions!' barked Mr Kidswatter.

'But don't worry, Eric,' he said gently. 'You have nothing to fear. So long as you tell the truth.' He cracked his knuckles.

Eric Ovens was very scared. Mrs Jewls always said that there was more than one answer to every question. He hoped he gave Mr Kidswatter the right ones.

'Did you have a spelling test last Friday?' Mr Kidswatter asked.

'Yes,' said Eric Ovens. 'How did you know that?'

'I have my ways,' Mr Kidswatter said slyly, behind his mirrored glasses. 'When was the last time you sharpened your pencil?'

'This morning,' said Eric Ovens. 'Maurecia accidentally stepped on it and –'

'Did you play kickball yesterday at a quarter after twelve?'

'No, I played tetherball.'

'Right- or left-handed?'

'Right.'

Mr Kidswatter tossed a stapler at him.

Eric caught it with his right hand.

Mr Kidswatter scowled. 'OK, Eric, tell me this. Have you ever gotten your hair cut at Charley's Barber Shop?'

'No, but I will. I'll go right now if you want.'

'You're not going anywhere!' shouted Mr Kidswatter. 'Have you ever heard of a Mugworm Griblick?'

Eric Ovens screamed.

Upstairs, Mrs Jewls heard Mr Kidswatter's voice resound over the loudspeaker.

'MRS JEWLS, SEND ME THE LAST ERIC!'

'On my way!' said Eric Bacon. He hopped out of his chair and bounced down the stairs.

He didn't bother knocking on Mr Kidswatter's door. He just walked right in. 'What can I do for you?' he asked.

There was no sign of Eric Ovens.

'Have a seat,' said Mr Kidswatter. 'I just want to ask you a few questions.'

'Sure thing,' said Eric Bacon. He sat in the little chair. He leaned back with his hands behind his head and his feet up on Mr Kidswatter's desk.

He looked at himself in Mr Kidswatter's mirrored glasses, took a comb out of his back pocket, and combed his hair. His hair was very neat and trim. He had got it cut yesterday, at 12:15, at Charley's Barber Shop.

Mr Kidswatter cracked his knuckles. 'When's the last time you sharpened your pencil?' he asked.

'November eleventh,' Eric Bacon answered right away. 'It was three minutes before five o'clock in the afternoon. I remember because my watch stopped.'

'Where were you yesterday at twelve-fifteen?'

'I was in the garden, having tea.'

'Did Maurecia step on somebody's pencil this morning?' asked Mr Kidswatter.

'Yes.'

'Whose?'

'She stepped on everybody's pencil,' said Eric Bacon.

'Are you left-handed or right-footed?' demanded Mr Kidswatter.

'I write with my left foot, and I kick with my right hand,' replied Eric Bacon.

Mr Kidswatter scowled. 'Have you ever gotten your hair cut at Charley's Barber Shop?'

'No, I never get my hair cut,' said Eric Bacon. 'I'm bald. This is a wig.'

Mr Kidswatter took off his glasses and glared at him. 'Do the words "Mugworm Griblick" mean anything to you?'

Eric Bacon shook his head. 'I can look it up in the dictionary if you want.'

Mr Kidswatter shook his head. 'I tried that,' he said. 'It's not there.' He rubbed his chin. 'OK, boys, you can come out now.'

Eric Ovens and Eric Fry crawled out from under the desk.

Mr Kidswatter looked at each Eric. 'One of you is lying,' he said. 'I don't know who it is, but I'll find out. And when I do, whoever it is will be very sorry. Now I'll give you one last chance to come clean.'

Eric Fry trembled.

Eric Ovens shivered.

'C'mon, let's blow this Popsicle stand,' said Eric Bacon. He walked out of the room. The other two Erics followed.

Mr Kidswatter rubbed the back of his neck. He looked at the white card on top of his desk. On one side it said:

CHARLEY'S BARBER SHOP

Under that, in blue ink, it said:

Eric, Tuesday, 12:15

He turned the card over. On the other side, a left-handed person had written with a sharp pencil:

Mr Kidswatter is a mugworm griblick

23

TEETH

Something terrible happened. Rondi grew two new front teeth.

Rondi was afraid nobody would think she was cute any more.

Mrs Jewls was giving a health lesson. 'Always brush your teeth,' she said, 'and remember to scrub behind your ears.'

'But I'll get toothpaste in my ear!' exclaimed Todd.

Everyone laughed. Except Rondi. She didn't want anybody to see her teeth. She hadn't smiled for a week.

Mrs Jewls made Todd write his name on the board under the word DISCIPLINE.

At recess Rondi decided to tell Louis her problem.

Louis was talking to Deedee.

'Do you have any green balls left?' asked Deedee.

'I'm sorry, I've already given them all away,' said Louis.

'That's not fair!' said Deedee. 'Why don't you ever save one for me?'

'You know I can't do that,' said Louis. 'If I save a ball for you, then all the other kids will want me to save balls for them, too.'

'Thanks for nothing, Louis!' said Deedee. She stormed away.

It was Rondi's turn. She made sure nobody else was listening. 'Louis, will you help me?' she whispered.

'Sure, Rondi, what's the problem?' asked Louis. Rondi smiled, showing Louis her teeth.

'Very nice,' said Louis.

'And listen to this,' said Rondi. 'She sells seashells by the seashore.'

'Very good,' said Louis.

'No it isn't!' complained Rondi. 'I used to whistle when I said words with *s*'s in them. Now nobody will think I'm cute.'

'I think you're cute,' said Louis.

'You don't count,' said Rondi.

'Well, thanks a lot,' said Louis.

'I didn't mean it bad,' said Rondi. 'You think every-body's cute, even Miss Mush! That's why I like you.'

'Thank you, Rondi. I like you, too.'

'Thank you,' said Rondi. 'Will you please kick me in the teeth?'

'No,' said Louis.

'Why not?' asked Rondi. 'You said you liked me. If you liked me, you'd kick me in the teeth.'

'You know I can't,' said Louis. 'If I kick you in the teeth, then all the other kids will want me to kick them in the teeth, too.'

Rondi scowled. 'Thanks for nothing, Louis!' she said. She crawled into the bushes where nobody would be able to see her mouth.

'Louis! Louis!' shouted Stephen and Jason as they ran towards him.

'Terrence stole our ball!' said Jason.

'I wish you children would learn to share,' said Louis.

'Make him give it back!' said Stephen.

Louis started to say something, then stopped. He twirled his multicoloured moustache. 'Hey, Rondi,' he called. 'Will you help me?'

Rondi crawled out of the bushes. 'You wouldn't help me,' she said. 'Why should I help you?'

'Terrence stole their ball,' said Louis. 'Make him give it back.'

'Her?' asked Stephen and Jason.

'Me?' asked Rondi.

Louis winked at her.

Rondi's eyes lit up. 'OK, Louis,' she said. 'That's a good idea. That's a wonderful idea!'

She hurried across the playground. Stephen and Jason ran after her.

Terrence kicked a red ball up into the air, then ran under it and caught it.

'Hey, Terrence!' said Rondi. 'That's not your ball. You stole it!'

'Drop dead, Ketchup Head,' said Terrence.

Rondi walked up to him, stared him straight in the eye, and said, 'In your hat, Muskrat!'

That surprised Terrence. He took a step back. Then he collected himself and said, 'Dig a hole, Milly Mole!'

Rondi took another step towards him. 'Kiss a goose, Dr Seuss!' she replied.

Terrence looked around. A group of kids had formed a circle around them. 'Go to jail, Garbage Pail!' he said.

Rondi held her ground. 'Go to the zoo, Mr Jagoo!' she retorted.

Everyone was very impressed by how brave Rondi was.

'Now, give me the ball!' she demanded.

'You want it?' asked Terrence. 'I'll give it to you all right!' He raised his fist in the air.

'Good, let me have it!' said Rondi. She smiled, showing him her two new teeth.

Terrence shook his fist at her. 'You're asking for it,' he said.

'That's right!' said Rondi. 'I am.' Her teeth gleamed at him.

Terrence brought his fist way back behind him.

Rondi closed her eyes.

'Hey, look!' exclaimed Bebe. 'Rondi's got new teeth!'

'They're cute,' said Jenny.

Rondi opened her eyes. 'You think so?' she asked.

'No, you were cuter before,' said Paul.

'I think she's cuter now,' said Todd.

They took a vote. Twelve kids thought she looked cuter with her two new teeth and twelve thought she looked cuter before. Three thought she should keep just one tooth.

So Rondi decided to keep her teeth. They were good for biting carrots.

'Uh-oh!' She suddenly remembered.

She ducked just in time.

24

ANOTHER STORY ABOUT POTATOES

Joe was next in line. He had forgotten his lunch.

'And what would you like, Joe?' asked Miss Mush.

'What do you have?' Joe asked.

'Potato salad,' said Miss Mush.

'Anything else?' asked Joe.

'No, just potato salad,' said Miss Mush.

Mrs Jewls had made Miss Mush throw away the rest of the Mushroom Surprise, and she made Miss Mush promise never to make it again.

'OK, I'll have potato salad,' said Joe.

Miss Mush smiled. She scooped a large glop of potato salad out of the vat and plopped it on Joe's paper plate.

Sharie was next in line. She had also forgotten her lunch.

'And what would you like, Sharie?' asked Miss Mush.

'What do you have?' asked Sharie.

'Potato salad.'

'What else is there?' asked Sharie.

'Nothing,' said Miss Mush.

'OK,' said Sharie. 'I'll have that.'

'Potato salad?' asked Miss Mush.

'No, nothing,' said Sharie.

Joe was the only one who ordered the potato salad. Everyone else ordered nothing.

He slid his paper plate over to the cash register and paid for his lunch. Then he went to the ketchup and mustard table.

He looked at the greyish-white mound on his plate. He thought it needed more colour. He squirted squiggly lines of mustard all over it. Then he added several dollops of red ketchup.

'That's very pretty, Joe,' said Bebe. 'I didn't know you were such a good artist.'

'Thanks,' said Joe. He looked for a place to sit.

'Hey, Joe! Over here!' called John.

Joe sat next to him. 'Hi, pal,' he said.

'Hi, good buddy,' replied John.

They were best friends.

John had brought his lunch. He looked at Joe's potato

salad covered with yellow squiggles and red polka dots. 'That's very colourful,' he said.

'Thanks,' said Joe.

They both stared at it.

'I wonder what it tastes like,' said John.

'Who knows?' said Joe.

'There's plenty more potato salad!' called Miss Mush. 'Who wants seconds?'

Nobody wanted seconds of potato salad. Several kids went back for seconds of nothing, but soon Miss Mush ran out of nothing.

Finally Joe picked up his plastic fork and stuck it into the glop.

'What does it feel like?' asked John.

'Lumpy and gooey,' said Joe. He dragged his fork over the mound, swirling the mustard and ketchup together. 'Kind of spongy, too.' The colours mixed with the potato salad. It turned a pale orange.

'It looks like a face,' said John.

Joe laughed. He shaped it so it would look even more like a face. He piled up some potato salad in the centre, giving it a nose.

John had a plastic spoon. He dug out two holes for the eyes, then made eyebrows.

'That's good,' said Joe. He gave it a big smiling mouth.

John made long, pointy ears.

They both laughed at their creation.

'I wonder what it tastes like,' said John.

'Who knows?' said Joe.

They stared at it.

'It kind of looks familiar,' said John. 'Like somebody I know.'

'Who?' asked Joe.

'I'm not sure,' said John.

Joe noticed it, too. 'It does look familiar,' he agreed.

'I've seen that face somewhere before,' said John.

'Me too,' said Joe.

The smile on the potato salad abruptly turned into a frown.

'Wow, did you see that?' asked Joe.

John's eyes filled with terror. 'I − I just figured out who it looks like,' he whispered.

'Who?' asked Joe.

'Mrs Gorf.'

The potato salad laughed.

'Ha! Ha! Ha!' said Mrs Gorf. 'Now I'll get you! You think you're so cute, don't you! Well, you won't get away from me this time!'

She wiggled her ears, first her right one, then her left.

'Quick, Joe!' said John. 'Eat her!'

The two boys dug their plastic utensils into the potato salad and shovelled it into their mouths as fast as they could.

Joe swallowed the final mouthful.

'Whew!' said John. 'That was close.'

Joe rubbed his belly and sighed.

They both stared at the empty plate.

'You know, Joe,' said John, 'that didn't taste too bad.'

'It was pretty good,' Joe agreed.

They went back for seconds.

25

A STORY THAT ISN'T ABOUT SOCKS

It was class picture day. The children were all dressed up in their best clothes.

Stephen came to school wearing a three-piece suit: grey trousers, a grey vest, and a grey jacket. Underneath his vest was a white shirt and a red-and-gold-striped tie. On his feet were hard, black, shiny shoes.

He was very handsome.

The other kids laughed when they saw him.

'You've worn lots of silly costumes,' said Bebe, 'but this is the silliest one yet!'

Bebe was wearing yellow shorts, a red shirt with white polka dots, and a floppy green hat.

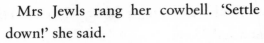

Mrs Jewls rang her cowbell. 'Settle down!' she said.

The children settled in their seats. Stephen remained standing.

'Look at Stephen,' said Maurecia. 'His jacket is the same colour as his pants.'

'They're supposed to be the same colour,' Stephen tried to explain. 'It's a suit. And they're not called pants, they're called *trousers*.'

'Oooooooh,' said Maurecia. 'Can you go swimming in your suit?'

'No,' said Stephen.

'I can go swimming in my suit,' said Maurecia.

Maurecia had on a black-and-white-striped bikini.

'I'm sure Stephen's suit is good for other things,' said Mrs Jewls.

'It is,' said Stephen.

'Like what?' asked Todd.

'Standing around and looking important,' said Stephen.

'What about sitting?' asked Todd.

'No, I'm not supposed to sit,' said Stephen. 'The suit might get wrinkled. I'm just supposed to stand around and look important.'

'Oh,' said Todd.

Todd was wearing white shorts, a Hawaiian shirt, and sunglasses.

Deedee crawled across the floor to Stephen so she could get a better look at his shoes. 'They're so shiny!' she said. 'I can see myself.' She knocked on one of his shoes with her fist. 'They're hard, too!'

'Deedee, get up,' said Mrs Jewls.

Deedee stood up. She had on a black T-shirt that came down to her knees. In the middle of the shirt was a red heart. Above the heart in sparkling silver and gold letters it said LOVE GODDESS.

'I bet they're good for kickball, huh, Stephen?' she asked. 'Since they're so hard.'

'No,' said Stephen. 'I can't run in them. And they hurt my feet.'

'Then why do you wear them?' asked Deedee.

'Because they're uncomfortable,' Stephen explained. 'You have to wear uncomfortable shoes if you want to look important.'

'Oh,' said Deedee.

'What's that thing around your neck?' asked Paul.

'It's a tie,' said Stephen.

'Does it keep your neck warm?' asked Paul.

'No,' said Stephen.

'Does it hold your shirt on?' asked Paul.

'No,' said Stephen.

'Well, what's it for?' asked Paul.

'It chokes me,' said Stephen.

'Oh,' said Paul.

'The more it chokes me, the better I look,' Stephen explained. 'See?' He tightened his tie.

'Oh, yeah,' said Paul. 'You look real handsome.'

Paul was wearing cowboy-and-Indian pyjamas.

Stephen pulled his tie tighter. 'Now how do I look?' he asked.

'Wow, you look great!' said D.J. 'Pull it tighter!'

Stephen pulled his tie even tighter. 'How's this?' he gasped.

'You look great and very important,' said D.J.

D.J. was wearing a toga made out of his bed sheet.

'Pull it tighter!' said Bebe.

Stephen pulled on his tie. He could no longer breathe.

'Tighter!' everyone yelled.

Stephen pulled it even tighter. His eyes bulged and his nose turned blue. He had never been more handsome.

'Tighter!' they all shouted.

Stephen pulled his tie so hard that he ripped it in half.

'Ohhhhhhhhh,' the whole class groaned.

'Darn!' said Stephen. 'Now I'm not great and important any more.'

'Yes you are, Stephen,' said Mrs Jewls. 'You're just as great and important as you ever were.'

'I am?' Stephen asked.

'Certainly,' said Mrs Jewls. 'The tie didn't make you

important. It doesn't matter what you wear on the outside. It's what's underneath that counts.'

'Underneath?' asked Stephen.

'Yes,' said Mrs Jewls. 'If you want to be great and important, you have to wear expensive underpants.'

'Oh,' said Stephen.

Mrs Jewls had on a flowered tank top and a grass skirt.

26

THE MEAN MRS JEWLS

Everybody in Mrs Jewls's class thought she was a very nice teacher.

They were wrong. There is no such thing as a nice teacher.

If you think you have a nice teacher, then you are wrong too.

Inside every nice teacher there is a mean and rotten teacher bursting to get out. The nicer the teacher is on the outside, the meaner the teacher inside is.

As Mrs Jewls was changing the bulletin board before class, a mean and rotten voice whispered inside her brain. 'Give the children lots of busy work today,' it said. 'And then make them do it over again if their handwriting isn't perfect.'

Mrs Jewls tried very hard to ignore the voice. She didn't like giving busy work. Instead she tried to teach the children three new things every day. She believed that if they learned three new things every day, they would eventually learn everything there is to know.

There are some classes where the teachers give so much busy work that the children never learn anything.

'What do you care if the children learn anything?' asked the mean and rotten voice. 'It's not your job to teach them. It's your job to punish them. Keep them in at recess. Hit them with your yardstick!'

The bell rang and all the kids scurried to their desks.

'We are going to learn three new things today,' Mrs Jewls announced. 'How to make pickles, seven plus four, and the capital of England.'

All the children paid close attention.

'The capital of England is London,' said Mrs Jewls. 'Seven plus four equals eleven. And pickles are made by sticking cucumbers in brine.'

On her desk she had a box of cucumbers and a vat of brine for a demonstration.

'OK, Joe,' said Mrs Jewls. 'How much is seven plus four?'

Joe shrugged.

'But I just told you, Joe,' said Mrs Jewls. 'Weren't you listening?'

'I don't know,' said Joe.

'OK, who can tell me how pickles are made? Yes, Jason.'

'Eleven!' Jason declared.

Mrs Jewls frowned. 'That's a correct answer,' she said, 'but unfortunately I didn't ask the right question. Can anyone tell me how pickles are made? Yes, Bebe.'

'In London,' said Bebe.

'I suppose they make some pickles in London,' said Mrs Jewls. 'OK, let's start again. Calvin, what's the capital of England?'

'Could you write England on the board?' asked Calvin. 'I can do a lot better when I can see the question.'

Mrs Jewls wrote *England* on the board.

'Oh, OK,' said Calvin, now that he saw the question. 'The capital of England is E.'

'Yes, that's one capital of England,' Mrs Jewls had to admit. 'OK, I will say it one more time. The capital of England is London.'

'Isn't that where they make all the pickles?' asked Jenny.

'No, they don't make all the pickles in London,' explained Allison. 'Just eleven.'

'Well, where do they make the rest of the pickles?' asked Stephen.

'Shut up!' shouted Mrs Jewls. 'Well, that does it. You're all staying inside for recess!'

Everyone stared at her. Mrs Jewls had never told anyone to shut up. It was against the class rules for anyone to use that expression. If you did, you had to write your name on the blackboard under the word DISCIPLINE.

Mrs Jewls put her hand over her mouth, then took it away. 'Oh dear, I'm very sorry,' she said. 'I don't know what came over me.'

She wrote her own name on the blackboard under the word DISCIPLINE.

'Perhaps you'll learn the lesson better if you write it down,' she suggested. 'Everyone please take out a piece of paper and a pickle.'

Everybody laughed.

'Pencil!' snapped Mrs Jewls. 'I meant to say pencil. It just came out pickle.'

'I didn't know pickles came from pencils,' said Jenny. 'I thought they came from cucumbers.'

'I thought they came from London,' said Todd.

Mrs Jewls made an ugly face. 'Todd, didn't I just tell you to shut up?' she asked. She picked up her yardstick and held it over Todd's head. 'Well, answer me!' she demanded. 'Didn't I tell you to shut up?'

'Yes,' said Todd.

'How dare you talk back to me!' snapped Mrs Jewls. 'Didn't I just tell you to shut up?'

Todd kept his mouth shut.

'Well, answer me!' she demanded.

Todd didn't know what to do. He nodded his head.

'Keep still!' ordered Mrs Jewls. 'Now I don't want you to say another word, is that clear?'

Todd stared at her.

'Is that clear?' she asked again.

'Yes,' Todd said meekly.

Mrs Jewls slammed down the yardstick. Todd quickly moved out of the way. The yardstick banged against his desk and broke in half.

Mrs Jewls stared at the eighteen inches she held in her hand. 'Oh my goodness,' she said. 'I'm sorry, Todd. I don't know what's the matter with me today. I must have gotten up on the wrong side of the bed this morning.'

She put a tick next to her name under the word DISCIPLINE.

'OK, let me try to make this very simple,' she said. 'If I have seven cucumbers. And then I get four more cucumbers. And then I drop all the cucumbers in brine and take them to the capital of England. What do I have? How many? And where am I?'

'Huh?' said D.J.

'What?' asked John.

'Could you write the question on the board, please?' asked Rondi.

'Shut up!' Mrs Jewls yelled a third time. In a mocking voice she said, '"Could you write the question on the board, please?" You kids think you are so cute! Well, we'll see just how cute you really are.' She picked up the vat of brine from her desk. 'How would you like it if I poured this on your heads? You won't be so cute when you're all shrivelled up and covered with warts, like pickles!'

She walked up and down the aisles carrying the pickle juice and glaring at the children.

No one dared make a sound.

She stopped next to Leslie. 'How about you, Leslie?' she asked. 'How would you like pickled pigtails?'

Leslie trembled. Her pigtails wiggled.

'Well, I'm going to ask you three questions, Leslie,' said Mrs Jewls. 'And if you don't answer them all correctly, I'm going to dump this on your head.'

Leslie gulped.

'Question one,' said Mrs Jewls. 'How much is seven plus four?'

Leslie quickly tried to count on her fingers but she didn't have enough. 'Eleven?' she guessed.

A look of disappointment came over Mrs Jewls's face. 'OK, question two: What is the capital of England?'

'L-London,' Leslie said nervously.

'Rats!' said Mrs Jewls. 'OK, question three.' She looked down at the vat of brine she was holding and shook her head. She thought a moment, then smiled. 'What is the name of my cousin who lives in Vermont?'

Leslie had no idea, so she just had to take a wild guess. She closed her eyes and said, 'Fred Jewls?'

'Wrong!' exclaimed Mrs Jewls. She raised the vat of brine high above Leslie's head and started to tip it over.

Paul jumped out of his seat. Those pigtails had once saved his life. Now it was his turn to return the favour!

He pushed the vat of brine back the other way. He was just trying to push it up straight, but he pushed too hard. It poured all over Mrs Jewls, drenching her.

Paul froze in terror.

Mrs Jewls blinked her eyes. Pickle juice dripped down her face. 'Thanks, Paul,' she said. 'I needed that.'

The brine had cured her.

She circled her name on the blackboard and sent herself home early on the kindergarten bus.

27

LOST AND FOUND

Joy and Maurecia were best friends. They sat down on the grass to eat their lunches, but then Maurecia remembered she needed chocolate milk. She went to get some from Miss Mush.

When she returned, she couldn't find her lunch.

'What happened to my lunch?' she asked.

Joy looked up at her, then shrugged her shoulders.

'I set my lunch down right here!' said Maurecia. 'You saw me, didn't you?'

Joy shook her head.

'I put it here, then I went to Miss Mush's room to get some chocolate milk. I had a peanut butter and banana sandwich! And there's no way I can eat a peanut butter and banana sandwich without chocolate milk.'

Joy shrugged her shoulders.

Maurecia didn't know what to do.

'Ca' I haf a thip uff your milk?' asked Joy.

It was hard for Joy to talk, because her mouth was full of peanut butter and bananas.

Maurecia handed Joy the carton of chocolate milk.

Joy took a big drink, then swallowed.

Maurecia looked all around for her lunch. She crawled in the dirt as she searched through the bushes.

'Any luck?' asked Joy as she finished Maurecia's chocolate milk.

'I found it!' Maurecia exclaimed.

Joy coughed on the chocolate milk. 'You did?' she asked, then coughed again.

Maurecia crawled out of the bushes holding a paper bag. She sat back down next to Joy and opened it.

'Is it your lunch?' asked Joy.

'No,' said Maurecia.

'Too bad,' said Joy.

'It's money!' exclaimed Maurecia.

Joy's eyes nearly popped out of her head as she looked at the paper bag. It was stuffed with dollar bills. And they weren't just one-dollar bills. There were a few five-dollar bills, some ten-dollar bills, but mostly twenty-dollar bills.

'We found a million dollars!' Joy whispered.

'We?' asked Maurecia.

They counted the money. It wasn't a million dollars. It was twenty thousand six hundred and fifty-five dollars.

'Let's split it,' said Joy. 'You take half and I'll take half.'

'Maybe I should show it to Louis,' said Maurecia.

'Louis!' exclaimed Joy. 'Are you crazy? Let's spend it. We can buy a skateboard, or a bicycle, or a horse, or a fancy car, or an aeroplane!'

'I like taking the bus,' said Maurecia.

'You could buy ice cream!' said Joy. 'All the ice cream you ever want for the rest of your life.' She knew Maurecia loved ice cream more than anything else in the world.

Maurecia smiled as she thought about it. 'No, I better show it to Louis. He'll know what to do.'

'You'll just get in trouble,' warned Joy. 'Louis will think you robbed a bank. You'll go to jail for the rest of your life.'

'Louis knows I'm not a bank robber,' said Maurecia.

'But what if the real bank robbers find out you have

their money?' asked Joy. 'They'll come after you and murder you.'

'Oh, I didn't think of that,' said Maurecia.

'You better give it to me,' said Joy.

'Louis will protect me,' said Maurecia. She walked across the playground.

Louis was talking to Terrence. He said, 'If you ever tie Leslie's pigtails to the tetherball pole again, I'll –'

'Louis, look!' said Maurecia. She held the paper bag up to his face.

'No thank you, Maurecia, I'm not hungry,' said Louis.

'It's not my lunch,' said Maurecia. 'Look inside!'

Louis took the bag from her and looked inside.

'Very nice,' he said, then gave it back to her. 'Now I want you to go untie Leslie and tell her –'

He suddenly stopped talking and blinked his eyes. He looked at Terrence, then at Maurecia, then at Terrence, then at Maurecia, and then at the paper bag. 'Let me see that again,' he said.

Maurecia gave him the bag.

'Hey, what about me?' asked Terrence.

'Get lost, Jack Frost,' said Louis.

Terrence ran away.

'Did you rob a bank?' asked Louis.

'No, I found it in the bushes,' said Maurecia.

'I believe you,' said Louis. 'We'll have to put it in the lost and found.'

'I know,' said Maurecia. 'Whoever lost it is probably very sad.'

'But if no one claims it in two weeks, you can have it,' said Louis. He took the bag of money and headed to the office.

Joy was waiting for Louis at the door. 'Hey, Louis,' she said. 'I lost a bag full of money. Have you seen it?'

'Help!' Leslie screamed from the tetherball court.

A week later, Maurecia was eating lunch alone. She was eating a piece of sweet potato pie. Joy was crawling around in the dirt looking for more bags of money.

'Maurecia,' said Louis, 'I'd like you to meet someone. This is Mr Finch.'

Mr Finch was an old man with white hair and a long white beard. He shook Maurecia's hand with both of his hands.

'It's your money, isn't it?' asked Maurecia.

Mr Finch nodded. 'It was my life's savings,' he said. 'For fifty years I made pencils. I got a penny for every pencil I made. I hate pencils! But finally I saved enough money to quit my job and do what I always wanted to do.'

'What's that?' asked Maurecia.

'I'm going to open my own ice-cream parlour,' he said, then started to cry. 'When I lost that money, I thought I'd have to start making pencils again.'

Maurecia cried too.

'Here, I want you to have this,' blubbered Mr Finch. He gave her an envelope containing five hundred dollars.

It was the second largest amount of money Maurecia had ever had.

'And I will give you free ice cream for the rest of your life at my ice-cream parlour,' he promised.

'Thank you!' said Maurecia.

'No, thank *you*,' said Mr Finch. 'I'm so glad someone as kind and as honest as you found it. There are so many dishonest people in the world. It's good to know there are still good people too.'

They hugged each other.

Joy crawled out of the bushes. 'Hey. Who's that?' she asked.

'This is Mr Finch,' said Maurecia. 'It's his money. Look, he gave me a reward of five hundred dollars. And I'll get free ice cream for the rest of my life!'

'Well, what about me?' Joy demanded. 'Don't I get anything?'

'Oh, dear me,' said Mr Finch. 'I didn't realise there was someone else involved.'

'Maurecia would never have found the money if it wasn't for me,' said Joy.

'Why, what'd you do?' asked Louis.

'I stole her lunch!' Joy said proudly.

Mr Finch gave her a pencil.

28

VALOOOSH

Mrs Jewls rang her cowbell. 'I have some wonderful news,' she said.

The children stopped what they were doing and looked up. They waited for Mrs Jewls to tell them the wonderful news.

'You are a very lucky class indeed,' said Mrs Jewls. 'Mrs Waloosh, the world famous dancer, will be coming here to Wayside School! She will teach you how to dance!'

Everyone was still waiting for the wonderful news.

'Isn't that exciting?' asked Mrs Jewls. 'You will see her every Wednesday instead of going to PE.'

'Will girls have to dance with *boys*?' asked Jenny.

'I suppose,' said Mrs Jewls.

'Gross!' exclaimed Leslie.

'Yuck!' said Dana.

'Will boys have to dance with *girls*?' asked Ron.

'Obviously,' said Mrs Jewls.

'No way!' said Eric Fry.

'I'd rather dance with a dead rat!' said Terrence. Everybody started talking at once – about cooties, and warts, and other horrible diseases you get from touching girls or boys.

Mrs Jewls rang her cowbell again and told them to settle down.

'Mrs Jewls, I don't need to take dancing lessons,' said Eric Bacon. 'I already know how to dance!'

'Yes, Eric, I've seen you "dance,"' Mrs Jewls said sarcastically.

Eric Bacon was a great breakdancer. But breakdancing was no longer allowed at Wayside School. That was because every time Eric danced, he broke something.

'Mrs Waloosh will teach you the grace and beauty of classical ballroom dancing,' said Mrs Jewls.

Everybody groaned.

On Wednesday they all headed down to their first dancing lesson. Except Myron. Myron went to PE.

'How come Myron never has to do anything?' asked Jason.

'I don't know!' said Calvin. 'I've been wondering about that too.'

'Myron's father must be friends with the president,' said Bebe.

'I think Myron gave Mr Kidswatter a thousand dollars,' said Todd.

'No, I bet he's blackmailing Mrs Jewls,' said Jenny.

'How could he do that?' asked Benjamin.

'Maybe Mrs Jewls got drunk!' said Jenny. 'And then she danced on top of her desk with a lampshade on her head. And Myron took her picture. And so now Mrs Jewls has to let Myron do anything he wants, or else he'll show the picture to Mr Kidswatter!'

'That makes sense,' said Mac.

'Except if she had a lampshade on her head, how would Mr Kidswatter know it was Mrs Jewls?' asked Todd.

No one knew the answer to that.

They entered the room on the second floor.

'Velcome!' said Mrs Waloosh, a strange-looking woman with bright red hair. It looked like her head was on fire. 'My name eez Meez Valoosh. It's so vonderful to be here at Vayside School.'

She wore pink tights and a sparkling pink top. 'I hope ve vill be friends, yes?' she asked.

Nobody said a word.

All around were red and green balls. There was also

one yellow ball. This was the room where Louis kept the balls for lunch and recess. It was also the room that was always used for school dances. It was the ballroom.

'So!' exclaimed Mrs Waloosh. 'Who vill be first?'

Everyone tried to hide behind someone else.

Mrs Waloosh put her hands on Ron's face. 'Vhat eez your name?' she asked.

'Ron,' he squeaked.

'RONALDO!' bellowed Mrs Waloosh. 'King of the Gypsies!'

'I don't know how to dance,' said Ron.

'D*ah*nce?' asked Mrs Waloosh. She looked very surprised. 'Ve are not going to d*ah*nce,' she said.

'We're not?' asked Ron.

'No, Ronaldo,' whispered Mrs Waloosh. 'Ve are going to *tango*!'

She put her left arm around Ron's waist. Then she grabbed his left hand with her right and stuck it way out in front of them. Suddenly the music started.

Mrs Waloosh dragged poor Ron across the room as she stomped her feet in time to the music.

Domp. Domp-domp. Domp-domp. Da-da-domp.

Domp! Domp! Domp! Domp! Domp-domp-domp-domp-domp, 'HEY!'

When she yelled 'HEY!' she threw Ron up in the air and clapped her hands. Ron turned a somersault in mid-air; then Mrs Waloosh caught him. They tangoed back to where they started. Ron's eyes were spinning in opposite directions.

'Hey, that looked like fun,' said Maurecia. 'Do me.'

'Very vell,' said Mrs Waloosh. She grabbed Maurecia and tangoed with her across the room. Domp. Domp-domp. Domp-domp. Da-da-domp. Domp! Domp! Domp! Domp! Domp-domp-domp- domp-domp, 'HEY!' She threw Maurecia up in the air and clapped her hands.

Maurecia turned a double somersault before Mrs Waloosh caught her. They tangoed back to the front.

'My turn,' said Terrance.

As Mrs Waloosh tangoed with Terrence, the other kids stamped their feet along with Mrs Waloosh. They all yelled 'HEY!' at the same time and clapped their hands.

One by one, Mrs Waloosh tangoed with every kid in the class. The other kids danced with each other. Boys danced with girls, and girls danced with boys. They didn't care. Paul danced with Leslie. Dana danced with John. Terrence danced with Rondi. Allison danced with Jason. D.J. danced with Kathy. Todd danced with Joy.

'HEY!' they all shouted together.

Of course, they weren't strong enough to throw each other up in the air. Instead, they tried to trip each other and throw each other to the ground. 'HEY!'

Even Kathy was having fun. 'HEY!' she shouted as she kicked D.J. in the rear end.

They also threw the balls at each other. 'HEY!'

Mrs Waloosh began to get tired. Sometimes she didn't catch the children after she tossed them in the air.

Deedee crashed to the floor. 'Wow,' she said, 'this is more fun than murder-the-man-with-the-ball! HEY!'

At last the music stopped. Domp! Domp! Domp! Domp! Domp-domp-domp-domp-domp. And everyone shouted 'HEY!' one last time.

Mrs Waloosh clapped her hands. 'Vonderful!' she exclaimed. 'Fahntasteek!'

They all staggered out of the ballroom, cut up, bruised, and bleeding.

'Next veek, ve valtz!' Mrs Waloosh called after them.

'So how did everyone like dancing?' asked Mrs Jewls when they returned.

'D*ah*nce?' asked Ronaldo, King of the Gypsies. 'Ve didn't d*ah*nce.'

'You didn't?' asked Mrs Jewls.

'No,' said Ronaldo. 'Ve *tangoed*!'

Everyone cheered.

'It vas vonderful!' exclaimed Kathy.

'Fahntasteek!' said Terrence.

Myron was sorry he had missed it.

'I can't vait till next Vednesday,' said Todd.

29

THE LOST EAR

Mrs Jewls was teaching the class about mammals. 'All mammals have hair,' she said.

Bebe raised her hand. 'Is my father a mammal?' she asked.

'Yes, all people are mammals,' said Mrs Jewls.

'But my father doesn't have any hair,' said Bebe. 'He's bald!'

Everybody laughed.

Benjamin stared down at his desk top. He was very determined. Mrs Jewls would be handing out report cards at the end of the week. He had to tell her his real name before then.

He raised his hand.

But Mac also had his hand raised.

'Yes, Mac,' said Mrs Jewls.

'I heard about a man who was getting his hair cut,' said Mac. 'And the barber cut off one of the man's ears! See, the man had very long hair. I think he was a hippie. So the barber couldn't see his ear until it fell on the floor.'

'Thank you, Mac,' said Mrs Jewls. 'That was a very interesting story.'

'I'm not finished,' said Mac. 'When the barber saw the ear on the floor, he said, "Is that your ear on the floor?" And then the hippie said "What? I can't hear you." So the barber showed him his ear; then he called an ambulance to take the hippie to the hospital.'

'Were they able to put his ear back on?' asked Todd.

'Well, see,' said Mac, 'the doctors were all set to sew it to his head. They were in the operating room and everything. But suddenly they couldn't find the ear. Man, they looked everywhere for it!'

'Did they look under the operating table?' asked Joy.

'Yep,' said Mac. 'It wasn't there.'

'How about in the bathroom?' asked Eric Bacon. 'Maybe they lost it when they washed their hands.'

'They looked, but it wasn't there,' said Mac.

'Did they leave it at the barber shop?' asked Jenny.

'Nope.'

'Did they ever find it?' asked Allison.

'Yes,' said Mac, 'but you'll never guess where!'

'In the refrigerator,' grumbled Mrs Jewls.

'No, how would it get there?' asked Mac.

'Well, we really need to get back to mammals,' said Mrs Jewls. 'Yes, Mark.'

Benjamin lowered his hand. 'My name's not Mark,' he said. 'My name really is Benjamin. Benjamin Nushmutt! And I came from Hempleton, not Magadonia.'

'Fine,' said Mrs Jewls. 'But we were talking about mammals. Now the whale is the largest mammal. Even though it lives in the ocean, it is still a mammal, not a fish.'

'Do whales have hair?' asked John.

'Yes,' said Mrs Jewls.

Dana laughed. 'A whale with pigtails!' she exclaimed.

'Boy, I'd love to pull one of those!' said Paul.

Benjamin couldn't believe it. 'Didn't you hear what I just said?' he asked.

'Yes, Benjamin,' said Mrs Jewls.

'Well, don't you think I'm strange?' asked Benjamin. 'All this time you've been calling me by the wrong name, and I never told you? Don't you think I'm crazy?'

'No,' said Mrs Jewls.

Benjamin was getting upset. 'Well, don't you think it's a stupid name? Benjamin Nush-mutt!' He looked around at his classmates. 'Doesn't anybody think I'm weird?'

'No, you're not weird!' said Sharie. 'I'll tell you what's weird. What's weird is bringing a hobo to school for show-and-tell. I'm the one who's weird.'

'That's not weird!' said Bebe. 'What's weird is telling everyone you have a brother when you don't. I'm the weirdo!'

'You call that weird?' exclaimed Stephen. '*I'm* weird. Who else would choke himself just to look nice?'

'That's not weird,' said Jenny. 'That's normal. Try reading a story backwards. That's weird. I'm the weird one in this class.'

'That's a laugh!' said Rondi. 'If you're so weird, then how come you never asked Louis to kick you in the teeth? I'm the one who's crazy!'

'No, that's not crazy,' said Todd. 'I'll tell you what's crazy. What's crazy is that we all go to school on the thirtieth floor, and the bathrooms are way down on the first!'

Everyone agreed with that, even Mrs Jewls.

Benjamin shook his head. What a bunch of weirdos! he thought. Then he smiled. He felt proud to be in a class where nobody was strange because nobody was normal.

'Oh, this must be your lunch,' said Mrs Jewls. She gave Benjamin the white paper bag that had been sitting on her desk since Benjamin's first day of school.

At lunch Allison headed down the stairs. 'Mark!' she exclaimed.

'Hi, Allison,' said Mark Miller. 'Long time no see.' He carried a white paper bag just like Benjamin's.

Allison was afraid she was back on the nineteenth storey.

'Don't worry,' said Mark. 'Suddenly everyone realised my name was Mark Miller and not Benjamin Nushmutt. And then Miss Zarves gave me this bag and told me to take it to the hospital.'

'Is it your lunch?' asked Allison.

'Look inside,' said Mark. He handed her the bag.

Allison looked inside.

There was an ear.

Allison's eyes lit up. 'Oh, now I get it!' she exclaimed. 'I understand everything! There is no Miss Zarves! See, Mac was talking about the ear, then Mark Miller, I mean Benjamin Nushmutt, said his name wasn't Mark Miller, so that means you –'

'What?' asked Mark.

Allison suddenly looked very confused. 'Never mind,' she mumbled.

For just a second Allison had understood everything, but then she lost it.

30

WAYSIDE SCHOOL IS FALLING DOWN

A strong wind whooshed around the playground in the early morning before school, blowing dirt and leaves in the faces of the children.

When the bell rang, they could hardly make it from the playground to the school. The wind was blowing directly at them, pushing their hair straight back.

With every gust of wind the school building teetered one way, then tottered back the other.

As they headed up the stairs, they could feel the building sway back and forth. The higher they got, the more it swayed.

'Hooray!' yelled Kathy. 'Wayside School is falling down!'

'What are you so happy about?' asked Joe. 'We'll all die.'

'Yes, but we won't have to do our homework,' said Kathy.

They entered the room on the thirtieth storey.

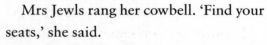 Mrs Jewls rang her cowbell. 'Find your seats,' she said.

That wasn't easy. All the desks were crammed together on one side of the room. The building swayed, and the desks slid to the other side of the room.

Finally the children all found their seats and planted their feet firmly on the floor.

'We are going to have a fire drill today,' Mrs Jewls told them. 'So let's be prepared. Who is our door monitor this week?'

'I am,' said Maurecia.

'Good,' said Mrs Jewls. 'Who is our help monitor?'

'I am,' said Jason.

'Very good,' said Mrs Jewls. 'You have a big mouth.'

Stephen raised his hand. 'What if there really is a fire?' he asked.

'There's not going to be a real fire,' said Mrs Jewls. 'It's just a drill.'

'I know, but what if there really is a fire?' asked Stephen. 'And then the firemen won't come because they'll think it's a drill! The school will burn down!'

'Don't worry,' said Kathy. 'The school is not going to burn down. It's going to fall down!'

BLEEP! BLEEP! BLEEP! ... BLEEP! BLEEP! BLEEP! ... BLEEP! BLEEP! BLEEP!

It was the fire drill.

Maurecia, the door monitor, held open the door.

Jason, the help monitor, ran to the window. 'Help!' he screamed. 'Save us! We're up here. Help! Help!'

Mrs Jewls led the children out of the room. If there was a real fire, the children might not be able to see her because of the smoke, so she constantly rang her cowbell. There wouldn't be time to go all the way down the stairs, either. Mrs Jewls led them up the ladder and through the trapdoor to the roof. If there was a real fire, helicopters would rescue them.

The wind was even worse on the roof than it was on the playground. Mrs Jewls stood in the centre and held the cowbell high above her head. She looked just like the Statue of Liberty.

'Everyone stay away from the edge!' she warned.

Kathy sang: 'Wayside School is falling down, falling down ...'

'It's not falling down,' said Stephen. 'It's burning down! And no one will rescue us because they think it's a drill.'

Jenny noticed a dark, funnel-shaped cloud off in the distance. 'Tornado!' she screamed. 'We're all going to get sucked off the roof!'

A flash of lightning lit the sky, followed by a loud crack of thunder.

'We're going to be struck by lightning!' shouted Todd.

'No we won't,' said Stephen. 'We'll burn in the fire.'

'No, we'll be sucked up in the tornado,' said Jenny.

'No, the school is going to fall down,' said Kathy.

Mrs Jewls continued to ring her cowbell. Klabonk! Klabonk! Klabonk! The strong wind carried the sound for miles.

Suddenly, screams came from down below. Then the whole building began to shake violently.

'Earthquake!' yelled Benjamin.

'Fire,' corrected Stephen.

'The school must have been struck by lightning,' said Todd.

'Tornado,' said Jenny.

'All fall down,' said Kathy.

The building continued to rumble and shake. There were more screams.

'Listen!' said Myron. 'They're trying to warn us about something.'

Down below, over five hundred kids and teachers were shouting together: 'STAR BRINGING PURPLE!'

'What are they saying?' asked Mrs Jewls.

'I don't know,' said Myron.

Mrs Jewls rattled her cowbell.

'STAR BRINGING PURPLE!' they shouted again.

'It sounds like "Star bringing purple,"' said Myron.

'What does that mean?' asked Mrs Jewls. Myron shrugged.

Mrs Jewls rang her bell even louder.

'STAR BRINGING YORBEL!'

'Wait,' said Myron. 'They're not saying, "Star bringing purple." They're saying, "Star bringing yorbel."'

'What's a yorbel?' asked Mrs Jewls. She rang her bell even louder.

The school shook and rumbled.

'STOP BRINGING YORBEL!'

'Stop something,' said Myron.

Mrs Jewls rang her cowbell.

'STOP RINGING YOUR BELL!'

'Stop ringing your bell,' said Myron.

'Oh,' said Mrs Jewls. She stopped ringing her bell.

Down below, all the students and teachers clapped their hands.

But it was too late.

Rondi opened the trapdoor. 'Cows!' she exclaimed.

The school was filled with cows.

From all over the countryside, cows had heard Mrs Jewls's cowbell and heeded the call. There were thousands of them. They filled the stairs and all the classrooms.

There was no way for the children to get down.

Helicopters finally came and took them one at a time off the roof.

Wayside School didn't blow down. It didn't burn down. It wasn't struck by lightning, sucked up in a tornado, or destroyed by an ear thquake.

It was cowed.

No one knew how to get rid of the cows. Cows are strange animals. They don't mind walking upstairs, but nothing can make them walk downstairs.

Someone suggested starving the cows, but the farmers wouldn't allow that. Thousands of bales of hay were sent in. Several cows had calves.

The newspapers thought it was funny and made jokes about smart cows learning to read and write.

And so Wayside School was closed. The kids and teachers were temporarily sent to different schools.

Only one person stayed behind. He was there all day and all night trying to get the cows to go home.

'C'mon,' pleaded Louis, the yard teacher, as he pushed and pulled on the cows. 'Go home. Please? Pretty please?'

Everybody mooed.

All sorts of crazy and unmissable things happen at Wayside School …

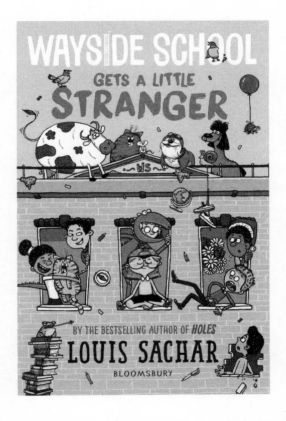

Read on for a sneak peek of the next book in Louis Sachar's side-splitting series

AVAILABLE NOW!

1

EXPLANATION

For two hundred and forty-three days, a lonely sign hung on the front of the old school building.

WAYSIDE SCHOOL CLOSED FOR REPAIRS

On some days a child would come, look at the sign, then sadly walk away.

Or else a child would come, look at the sign, stand on her head, then sadly walk away.

Louis watched them come and go.

But he never said 'Hi!' to them. He hid when they came.

It was his job to repair the school.

Louis used to be the yard teacher at Wayside School. He passed out the balls and played with the kids at recess and lunch.

When the school closed, the children were sent to other schools. Horrible schools. No two kids were sent to the same school.

Louis was afraid he'd cry if he talked to them.

But he worked hard. For two hundred and forty-two days, he pushed and pulled, shovelled and mopped. He never left the building. At night he slept on the couch in the teachers' lounge on the twelfth floor.

Some days it seemed hopeless. The worst part was the smell. He often had to run and stick his head out a window to get a breath of fresh air. But whenever he felt like quitting, he thought about those poor kids, stuck in those horrible schools, and he just worked harder.

And at last, two hundred and forty-three days later, the school was ready to open.

Well, almost ready. There was one little problem.

Suddenly, from somewhere inside the building, or maybe just inside his head, Louis heard a loud 'moo.'

He put his hands over his ears and said, 'I don't hear it, I don't hear it, I don't hear it,' until the mooing stopped.

He had scrubbed and polished every inch of Wayside School. There were no cows anywhere. He was sure of it! Still, every once in a while, he heard something go 'moo'. Or at least he thought he did.

He took the sign off the door.

But before you enter, you should know something about Wayside School.

Wayside School is a thirty-storey building with one room on each floor, except there is no nineteenth storey.

Mrs Jewls teaches the class on the thirtieth storey.

Miss Zarves teaches the class on the nineteenth storey. There is no Miss Zarves.

Understand?

Good; explain it to me.

'*Louis!*' someone shouted.

He turned to see a red and blue overcoat running towards him. 'Hi, Sharie!' he said. He couldn't see her face, but he knew she had to be somewhere inside the coat.

Sharie jumped into his arms.

'I bet you're glad to be back,' said Louis.

'You bet!' said Sharie. 'Now I can finally get some sleep!'

All around the playground, old friends were getting back together.

'Hi, old pal!' said John.

'Hey, good buddy,' said Joe.

'Bebe!' yelled Calvin from one side of the playground.

'Calvin!' shouted Bebe from the other.

They ran and smashed into each other.

'Hi, Eric, good to see you,' said Eric.

'Hey, good to see you too,' said Eric. 'Oh, look. There's Eric!'

'Hi, Eric! Hi, Eric!'

'Hi, Eric.'

'Hi, Eric.'

Even Kathy said hello to everybody.

'Hey, Big Ears!' she said to Myron as she slapped him on the back. 'What's happ'nin', Smelly?' she asked Dameon. 'You didn't take a bath for two hundred and forty-three days, did you? Hi, Allison. Did you get uglier while you were away, or were you always this ugly and I just forgot?'

'That's a nice sweater, Kathy,' said Allison, who always tried to say something nice.

Kathy moved on to Terrence. 'I'm sure glad to see you, Terrence!' she said.

'You are?' asked Terrence.

'Yes,' said Kathy. 'I thought you'd be in jail by now.'

Todd came running across the playground.

'Hi, Todd!' shouted Sharie, right in Louis's ear.

Todd kept running.

'Hey, Todd!' called Jason. 'Good to see you!'

'Hi, Todd!' called Myron and D.J.

But Todd didn't answer. He just kept running until he reached the school building.

Then he kissed Wayside School.

Out of all the schools, Todd had been sent to the very worst one. It was awful! The first thing he had to do every morning was—

Wait a second. I don't have to tell you. You already know.

Todd was sent to your school.

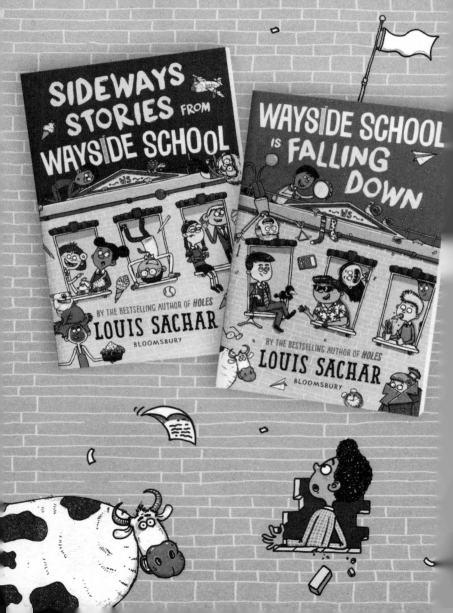

ABOUT THE AUTHOR

Louis Sachar is the author of the international bestseller and award-winning *Holes*, which was made into a film in 2003. All of Louis's books for children have been published in the UK by Bloomsbury. These also include *Small Steps*, *Stanley Yelnats' Survival Guide to Camp Green Lake*, *Dogs Don't Tell Jokes*, *There's a Boy in the Girls' Bathroom*, *Someday Angeline*, and the Marvin Redpost series and Wayside School books. Louis Sachar lives in Austin, Texas, with his wife, daughter and two dogs.

ABOUT THE ILLUSTRATOR

Aleksei Bitskoff was born in Estonia and graduated with a master's in Illustration from Camberwell College of Arts, London, in 2010. His influences include Russian illustrators and animators, as well as Tove Jansson and the Moomintrolls. Aleksei lives in London with his wife and their two children.